A
Witch's
Welcome

Sonia Taylor Brock

DEDICATION

In memory
Of my father
Robert John Taylor
May 17, 1939 – November 25, 2011

CONTENTS

1   Dan's Journal

2   It's a Fish!

3   You are So Busted!

4   A Pirate's Cruise

5   A Queen Awakens

6   Thelma and Louise in NOLA

7   Getting Ship Shape

8   Truths and Consequences

9   Water, Water, Everywhere

10   Alliances Carefully Forged

11   The Green-Eyed Monster

12   No Time for Lizard Boy

13   What Not to Wear

14   I'll Sip On Your Bones For My Supper

15   A Gauntlet Is Thrown

16   Like Water Rippling Outward

17   General Jamie in Command

18   Yayyy! Pirates!

19 A Witch Riding on a Killer's Back

20 Reunited at Last

21 The Tiny Ship was Tossed

22 A Dangerous Journey Through Cajun Country

23 A Masquerading Army

24 A Life for Life

25 An Eternity of Imprisonment

26 A New Balance of Power

27 Why Didn't You Do That Before?

28 Wyrms!

29 So You Want to Fight Dirty

30 The Bitch Bites

31 Blood Rained in Horror

32 Godzilla vs King Kong

33 A King Returns

34 A Love Lost

35 The Long Trip Home

36 Prologue

1 DAN'S JOURNAL

September 1, 2012

It started out as a beautiful day. The sun was shining. Birds were chirping. A cool breeze was gently blowing in from the Gulf. It felt great to be alive...until I tripped over a severed troll's leg, landing face first in goo from a dead vampire. Apparently there were still some areas of the little island the cleanup crews had not reached.

We completed the cleanup at Stella's house. Despite the devastating battle which occurred here a mere two days ago, it wasn't as bad as I thought it would be. Aside from my misstep into a rotting corpse.

It has been a little while since I have

updated this journal. I will begin with a short recap to organize my thoughts into proper perspective.

Alan Crowley, a sorcerer and direct descendent of the infamous Morgan Le Fey of medieval lore, waged war on Stella and her strange little family with a storm straight from Hell itself. He is now dead. He was definitively insane; as corrupted by evil and power as his ancestor had been centuries ago. Thankfully, his plot to organize an army of vampires and his crazy desire for power and control was stopped in its tracks.

His accomplices: a clan of greedy, bad tempered Boggarts led by Brady Bauchan and an army of fledgling vampires created by a mysterious unidentified master vampire who organized a group of Trolls being controlled by a few spells Bauchan dug up from some Old Fae magic legends. The Trolls and the vampires were used to execute Crowley's evil plan on several fronts.

The Mariner (see poem; Rhyme of the Ancient Mariner), the Father of all Vampires turned into a Vampire Hunter, was still trying to identify the mysterious Master Vampire and his origins. So far no trace of him has been found.

Brady Bauchan also escaped. He disappeared into the shadows of the world for the time being. Searches for his corpse proved fruitless in the aftermath of the conflict despite several reports of seeing him badly wounded, yet still alive.

It is still hard for me to fathom only three months ago I was living a very mundane life. I didn't think so at the time. I had been constantly scrabbling for the one story that would put my career on the fast-track. I only encountered mediocre success writing for the tabloids as an independent.

I also lived with a rare disability; a severe sensitivity to natural sunlight. No, not a form of vampirism, but an actual physical inability for my pupils to contract and filter sunlight. Though I am fair-skinned due to a lifetime of living indoors during the day, I realized recently I am beginning to have a semblance of a tan for the first time.

I will never forget the blinding epiphany (pardon the pun) of the exact moment I discovered what my disability really was and how to use it for its intended purpose. It would change everything about my life.

I am a supposedly powerful empath. My pupils didn't contract because they were trying to activate. My brain was struggling to receive images.

After meeting these strange people with special abilities, my dormant empathic ability, which had been blocked because I didn't know how to process the information I was receiving, was brought into acute focus when I met Stella. Stella and Jamie, both with telepathic abilities, helped me remove the mental blocks and assisted in recognizing my own God-given talent.

In that vein, let me digress for a moment; contrary to popular belief, these people and races are true believers of God and religions.

For if not, they would not exist at all. Some of them were spurned. As a direct result of those beliefs they continue to exist. Some, like Stella, are older than the Bible and other religious texts (depending on your particular faith). Many were actual witnesses of the events recorded within those texts.

There is more history pertaining to them than today's modern humans will ever be able to comprehend or accept; were they made aware of the enormity of it as a whole.

I am one of those lucky few chosen to be made aware of these missing items of history. I still consider myself human, only with an added skill; much like an athlete achieves Olympian status (tests confirm my human physiology has not been altered.)

I am recording my experiences and observations as an exercise in research, if you will, for a better understanding of each race I encounter and its intricacies. Where this will lead, I cannot say. My newfound intuition tells me it is vitally important I continue to make these records.

Back to recording my experiences...where was I? Oh yes. A whole new world had revealed itself to me. The stuff of old fairy tales and legends were now a major part of my life and as odd as it sounds, I am ok with it. A lifetime affliction of severe light sensitivity was fine tuned for its real purpose. For the first time in my life, I was going to see the world with my eyes wide open.

I can't begin to tell you the freedom I feel now. Not having to shield my eyes, wear sunglasses and being able to look skyward. My condition thoroughly trained me to keep my head down, stay inside and avoid direct sunlight. I was virtually held prisoner by my own body.

I guess my new freedom wasn't without its own pitfalls. By the current state of decomposition dripping down my pant leg, there would still be times I would need to look down to keep from stepping in something I couldn't get out of, so to speak.

At least there were no law enforcement officials we would have to explain as to why this tiny island was littered with dead monsters. I can just see it now. Stella looking up at the detective and telling him, "Mais yeah, Chere, dey was tresspassin on my property, so I fed em' to my gator."

It only took a couple of hours to clean up what was left of the bodies. The Nereids are an aquatic race of females that live in the ocean. Potomoi are their male counterparts and live in rivers and streams that run into the ocean. Oh, and by the way, never, ever call them mermaids if you value your testicles. It will be quickly and painfully explained to you that they are not manatees, nor are they animated whining Disney princess cartoons.

Anyway, they took care of what was left of the troll corpses. Troll corpses are difficult to dispose of because the density of their bodies. They do not burn. They decay extremely slowly. They have very little buoyancy. While the bodies were a problem on land, they provided excellent material to shore up the eroding reefs. This would provide excellent breeding grounds for the aquatic flora and fauna that inhabit this coastline.

The vampire bodies were a different problem entirely. There was not a single use for them. Even the Cajuns had no use for them, and their motto is, "they will eat anything that doesn't eat them first and it better put up a good fight".

A dead vampire who has not progressed past the pupae stage is much like an animated, hungry, puss filled sack of skin. The bodily fluids are extremely toxic and the smell is utterly nauseating. The smell alone really made you wish they dissolved into dust like in the movies we all watched as kids.

Vampire bonfires were the preferred means of disposal. What smells worse than a dead vampire? A dead, burning vampire. You become an expert in mouth breathing really fast. Even then, you can almost taste the rot. It was especially hard on Aundrea and the rest of the Weres. They have an amplified sense of smell. She actually vomited several times.

Repair efforts began immediately on Stella's home. I was amazed at how much could be done in such a short period of time. At Hawk's and Jamie's insistence, a generator and wiring were installed to provide the "unnecessary luxury," according to Stella, of electricity in the house. New sinks, fixtures and plumbing were added and the kitchen was updated under Stella's watchful eye. A new chef's style gas stove and oven, a sub-zero refrigerator/freezer unit complete with icemaker (the only thing besides her new shower that she was truly happy with), and even a dishwasher everyone was sure would remain unused.

With all the renovation, Justin, the general contractor as well as one of Hawk's sons, and a werewolf, decided the house needed to be enlarged as well. Another bathroom was added, complete with a shower that fed directly from the Gulf to Stella's bedroom, so she could "re-charge" quickly at her leisure. Her ability to re-charge inside her home caused quite a stir during the storm and measures were taken so she could do it inside should the need ever arise again.

The old back porch was transformed into a den that doubled as an armory to house some of Stella's more exceptional pieces of weaponry. Also, for the convenience of quick access in case of an attack. Stella insisted she have the use of a sink area for washing and cleaning game. As a result, an outdoor kitchen was constructed, complete with wash sink, gas grill and pergola. When seeing it completed, Stella made the comment it reminded her of the Greek style of entertaining centuries ago, but without slaves.

Scratchy watched everything with the concentration of a huntress stalking prey. Scratchy Patchy, or more appropriately, Bernice, was Stella's calico cat. She had one normal cat eye and one really weird human eye. Her rump was completely bald and callused from pulling her own hair out, resembling a baboon's butt. Most of her tail was bare and she only had several patches of fur on her little body. She was obsessed with cleaning herself. Stella constantly reassured her that she was flea free and the crawling sensation was only in her mind. Jamie was currently treating her for dermatitis and eczema. I guess even supernatural creatures can have that "not quite so fresh feeling."

I might add that Scratchy is also a Were person. Stuck in her animal spirit form, she has been traumatized and her mind is damaged. She cannot concentrate hard enough to change completely back, hence the one human eye. It is unsettling to look at her at first, but after a while she grows on you.

She is also Stella's assistant and treasurer; keeper of all things hidden. Which is why she was so agitated during all the improvements and cleanup. When something wasn't exactly right, she would attack the workers with her razor sharp claws and snapping teeth.

One time, she actually jumped on a worker, claws digging into his shirt and grabbed his sleeve in her mouth, digging deep with elongated fangs, and shook his arm to make him let go of a basket he had picked up.

When he dropped the basket in surprise, she simply jumped down, flicked her tail at him, grabbed the basket in her mouth and ran away. The man was bleeding in several places. Fortunately, he wasn't human and quickly healed the superficial wounds.

The workers quickly learned to defer to her *before* they changed anything. It was quite amusing, actually, to see big burly contractors consulting with a very small cat. They would look her direction before they touched anything and watch for any reaction. If she gave none they were safe, if her tail twitched and she flicked her ears, they put it back where it was and she would jump over and move it herself.

Once the cleanup and repairs were complete, our group began to disperse and go back to their lives as usual. It quickly became apparent I had a decision to make. My "job" here was done. I didn't know what to do next. I had come to the realization my old life was over. Stella must have sensed my feeling of loss and confusion. She told me not to worry about it. I would soon find my real purpose in the world and would be happier than I have ever been.

I wrote the story that brought me to this strange place and submitted it for publication. Not the story I thought I would be writing and certainly not the real story, but as MaMere put it, "the raht story".

The same day, Hawk called and told

me the board of directors for the school Jamie's girls attended called and wanted to meet with me regarding my article. They were impressed with the way I handled the delicate matter of explaining the difference of being a think tank exploiting kids with psychic abilities and a school that offered guidance for children that were challenged by added abilities or a lack thereof.

They offered me a position of director of public relations with a nice little salary to go along with it. Finally! A steady paycheck! They also told me to continue with my free-lance work because the greater accolades I got as a journalist increased my credibility with the press and added weight to my work with the school. I couldn't have asked for a sweeter deal.

As I left the conference room I noticed a wall was dedicated with the pictures of former members of the board of directors. There was one with a name plate of Robert Brown-Wing Eschte as chairman from years past. I guess it didn't hurt to have friends in the right places.

When I got back from Baton Rouge, I told everyone my good news. Jamie's girls whooped and cheered for me. Adey asked me in her usual stone-faced blunt style, "When are you going to move all your stuff?" I had been so excited about the opportunity it didn't occur to me I would have to give up my apartment in Los Angeles. I just stood there blinking at my oversight.

Jamie stepped up and said, "I am sure MaMere wouldn't mind having you stay here until you find a place of your own."

At that, Stella chimed in, "Chere, you is always welcome in mah home yeah. You stay as long as ya lahk."

That settled, everyone began to go about their daily business and I was left alone to think. I made my way via a passing shrimp boat (there are always people coming and going from this little island) to Lucky's restaurant, Benoit's. This was a habit I developed the moment I arrived in Louisiana.

What that man does with seafood is amazing. Five star chefs would have a hard time keeping pace with him. Although the dishes were prepared simply, they were delicious. I began to believe he could make your mouth water with a boiled tennis shoe. Now hopelessly addicted to the salty, dried shrimp that completely replaced usual appetizer fare, I popped them in my mouth and enjoyed an icy cold beer while listening to the local chatter that surrounded the diner.

Everyone here knew everyone else. There were old gossips, sure... but they actually cared about one another's families and well-being. Sitting here, you listened to the chatter from the fishermen and shrimpers after they finished their day and stopped in to drop off goods for the restaurant or to have a cold beer or two before they made their way home to their beds.

They weren't the only ones considered family here. There were roughnecks (oil rig workers), tradesmen, politicians, musicians, mothers with their children in tow and people from every walk of life. All making their way in this world and using this little place as a central meeting place for news. It was a getaway from home with a strong sense of community.

I loved this place with its easy, comfortable charm and began to marvel at how attached I had become. It's times like this I am amazed at how much my life has changed since I came to this strange place. No longer tense and anxious about what tomorrow might bring, I have begun to learn how to relax and appreciate simply having a good day.

Always the loner, I now had close friends. A lot of close friends that would lay down their lives for me if the situation arose. With the company I now keep, that is not just a fanciful thought, but a real possibility at any given moment.

I began to think how empty my life had been before. I truly thought that I was happy. In the past, I always felt there was something greater in life, but had come to accept the premise that in a man's life it was expected if you worked hard at doing something you were good at (whether you actually liked what you were doing or not), saved a little money and with any luck, in time, your greatest achievement would be to die without debt in a home of your own to pass on to your children.

Not only did I feel a sense of freedom from the affliction with my eyes, I felt free to explore new frontiers, new people-hell, even myself and what my newly discovered abilities might become. I was exhilarated. I also wanted to find out more about a certain woman who had been haunting my dreams all my life.

She was here - alive and uninhibited - and I think, into me. She is always keeping me off balance though. I feel the connection and the attraction but one minute she is making me hot and eager and the next moment she is questioning my masculinity.

I think my next course of action is going to be to make her a believer. I just have to find a way to get her alone for a little while.

2 IT'S A FISH!

It was Stella's devotion to her grandbabies that gave me the opportunity to get Jamie alone. She decided she and the girls were going to go into town and do a little shopping. "Deese girls is growin so fast, dey gittin too old to be wearin little girl's dresses."

Jamie started to argue with her when Maddie told her, "Come on Mom. Surely you've noticed we are growing into the bodies of young women now." Through Maddie's adult tone, and hearing Mom instead of Momma, Jamie reconsidered her first instinct to argue the point. She gave in and let them go with Stella with mixed emotions.

Stella, Sam, Aundrea and the girls all loaded up into the pirogue and set off for town. I noticed they were using Jean as a living outboard motor again. Jean was Stella's lover, and currently in the form of a humongous thirty foot alligator. She turned him into an alligator a long time ago because he couldn't control his jealous temper. She was also trying to teach him an important anger management lesson.

Joe, the local Sheriff and another of Hawk's sons, was a Were with a spirit animal of a cave bear. He told me he was constantly amused when MaMere went into town. She always took her pirogue, "Down da Bayou," and no one ever noticed there were no sounds of a motor!

Right before they took off, Stella called to Jamie and told her to go check the lines. When she got back she wanted to have some redfish and speckled trout for dinner. Jamie nodded and waved goodbye to them.

A little choked up, she turned to me and said "Come on Dan my man. We're goin' fishin." She went to the newly re-built garage in the back of the house and got fishing poles, tackle box, and two large buckets. Together, we hauled all the gear to a small beach past the swamp on the other side of the island.

Certainly you could call me a novice because fishing was an outdoor sport conducted in bright sunlight, a sport that had previously been on my list of unattainable things because of my affliction.

Jamie surprised me by patiently showing me how to rig my line, bait the hook, and cast. After several botched attempts, almost hooking her in the back of the ear once, then finally ending up with my line caught in an overhanging cypress tree, she gave up. She fashioned a cane pole she cut with her machete from a small patch of the bamboo growing nearby.

Embarrassed at my lack of coordination, I tried to apologize. She just shrugged and said, "Don't worry about it. We all did it when we were learning to fish. You don't get into your first car automatically knowing how to drive, do you? You have to learn how and practice until you have your coordination down."

I was surprised at her understanding and insight. I plunked my hook and bobber into the water and was somewhat consoled when I didn't get hooked or tangled in anything before I got the bait wet. After just a few moments, I was shocked to see the little bobber start bouncing in the water. I could actually feel the little tugs on the line through the pole.

Hearing my excited breathing, Jamie said softly, "Waaait for it. You don't want to pull hard until the cork goes completely under. That means he has taken the bait completely in his mouth and is trying to run with it."

I almost couldn't contain myself. I felt the little nibbles and almost jerked the line out of the water too early. Suddenly, just as she said, the fish jerked the cork under and ran. She yelled, "Now!" I jerked the line so hard I flung the fish completely out of the water and onto the bank. It was flopping all over the place. I was so excited I was screaming like a little kid, "I did it! I did it! It's a fish!"

Jamie chuckled. "Yes, you did great!

It's a nice sized speckled trout, not bad for your first time!"

Louisiana is truly a fisherman's paradise, no matter how bad a fisherman you are.

I looked at her and said, "Now what do I do with it?"

She laughed out loud this time and said, "You take the hook out and put it on the stringer, dummy."

I just stood there, holding the pole, and glared at her.

She chuckled; she had been teasing me again. She finally got up, went over to the fish and picked it up.

She showed me how to hold it under the gills so the spines on the fins wouldn't stick me in the hands. She then instructed me how to hold the line and follow it to the hook in the mouth and disengage the hook. Next, she showed me how to thread the pointed end of the stringer into its mouth and out through the gill. She tied the stringer to a tree and threw the stringer and the fish back into the water to keep my fish alive until we were done fishing.

We fished for a little while. I watched as Jamie busied herself with the task of catching fish. Because she could cast her line out further than I could, her chances of getting bigger fish were greatly increased. She rarely had to wait more than ten minutes before she had a bite on her line. I asked her what her trick was.

She looked at me like I had grown a third head. She then closed her eyes, searching for patience, and told me she used fishing as a mind exercise. She explained how she would open her mind, or as Stella told her, the third eye, and feel for the presence of life all around her.

With practice, she said she learned to distinguish what kinds of life she sensed below the water's surface. Therefore, when she detected a larger group of fish in the area, she would cast her line in the direction they were circulating. The rest was up to patience and skill, just like any other fisherman.

She explained her senses only gave her a slight edge and anyone with an electronic fish finder would have the same advantage. She told me you can lead a horse to water, but you can't make him drink. It is the same with fish, you can put the bait in front of them, but you can't make them take it.

She told me to follow her example, close my eyes and find my center. Then reach out and try to sense the life around me. Figure out what different kinds of life I could detect. I plunked my hook in the water, got still, and relaxed.

I listened and "saw" the little insects in my mind all around us. I thought to myself anyone with good hearing could do that, so then I listened harder and began to detect the different types of birds. In the trees I could hear their little hearts beating so quickly. I also sensed the larger ones off in the distance. I began to really see and understand what they were doing. There was a dove in the branches of the tree above my head. She was calling for her mate. There was a nest and she was hungry. I began to feel the little bird's thoughts; it was his turn to tend the nest and she was getting impatient. When I realized I could fully understand them, I was so shocked I lost my focus. I jumped a little and Jamie just smiled in understanding. She told me to focus on the water now.

I gazed at the water and felt myself start to relax again. I opened myself up to the feelings surrounding me. I felt the softness of the little waves lapping at each other, the sunlight sparkling on the surface. I began to feel my thoughts slip beneath the water. I found that I could see scurrying crabs and shrimp marching across the bottom, oysters and shimmering curtains of tiny minnows, an eel and a turtle. I could see the larger fish she told me she had been tracking. I began to know what kinds of fish they were.

Intrigued, I felt a little deeper and further. I discovered some of the troll corpses we fought with when the attack on Stella's island first began. I saw the remains where Sam blew up their boat and Jean had attacked them underwater. I shuddered with the thought of the bodies still being there but kept going. I found sunken boats, underwater caves, a large stingray, two small sand sharks, and something else, something bigger, almost humanoid.

I first thought that I had found a Nereid, but was surprised to feel it was a male presence. He was watching something very carefully and wasn't happy about it. I got the distinct impression that it was about an invasion of territory. Further off, a large shape loomed on the bottom of the Gulf. Getting closer, I discovered it was Max having a nap.

When I realized who it was, I reached out to him. I told Max about the other being. He yawned and stretched, blowing a huge spray of bubbles and clouding the whole area in a blanket of silt. He told me the local inhabitants, namely Nereids and Potomoi, were not accustomed to having dragons in their gardens and were a little upset.

In fact, these brackish waters are the only place the two types of creatures come into contact with each other. The Potomoi could tolerate only a little salt and the Nereids have to have just enough to survive. I told him from the thought impressions I got coming off that male, they were mad because they thought he was scaring the fish away from the hunting grounds and heating up the water too much.

He gave me a mental shrug and stretched again like a cat. He got up and swam a little farther off to make the Potomoi male happy and continue his nap in peace. Amused at his predicament, I watched him grumble and swim away. I think Jamie must have been monitoring the situation. I noticed a distinct smirk on her face.

We both began to let go and just

relax, watching the water. We stayed that way for some time when she finally broke the silence and asked if I had thought about where I might relocate to and when.

To be honest, I didn't know the area that well and told her so. I told her I would eventually have to find a place convenient near the school. She nodded and told me before her husband died, they had a house together not very far from the school. It was paid for and vacant at the moment. She offered to let me stay there if I liked.

I asked why she didn't live there herself. She told me she tried after he died, but it held too many bad memories and the location would make it too tempting to see the girls all the time. It would definitely arouse suspicions in several dangerous beings.

Noticing the pain in her eyes, I said she must have loved him very much. She smiled and said it had been part puppy love, part rebellion. She wanted to be her own person; independent and carefree. Besides, it was a thrill for a young girl to catch an older, attractive man's eye. At the time she thought she was in love. Shortly after they were married settled into daily life, she found the older, handsome, mysterious man was just an ordinary guy. He worked hard, came home, drank his beer and watched football. They really had nothing in common other than being not of the human variety. He was a werewolf.

Sure, he was good in bed and she enjoyed him. Over time she realized she wasn't really happy with being just a wife and mother, washing laundry and cooking dinner. She wanted more out of life.

Before the accident, he told her he knew that she wasn't happy and suggested she go to school to find out if there was something else that would make her feel more complete. She did say he was never mean or abusive. He was just a REALLY ordinary guy. Having been raised with such colorful characters at Old Lady Lake, she was bored. She said she knew it sounded awful, but she couldn't help it. She always felt guilty about it.

After the girls went missing and she got away from the boggarts, she never went back to the house they had shared. She hired people to maintain the property. They kept it clean and in good shape. She rented it out for a while to a single mother and her son. They lived there until the son went off to college and the woman eventually died.

Puzzled, I said, "Wait, if you could afford to hire people to keep up the house and he worked hard for a living, I don't mean to pry and maybe it's the reporter in me, but did I miss something? I thought the two of you had very little money." She laughed outright, "You humans. You always assume when you hear of people who work hard they have nothing. That may be true of most humans starting out, but we have lived many centuries and have accumulated many things over the years, including money. I never said the house was small!"

This made me realize I never asked her how old she was. She saw the look in my eye and stopped me before I began. "You know it's not polite to ask a lady her age." I closed my mouth with a pop, swallowing the question.

I told her if it didn't bother her to have me in the house, it might be the solution I was looking for and thanked her for her generosity. I waited a minute or two before I continued, "And since you know exactly where it is I hope you will be a frequent visitor if the memories aren't too bad."

She smiled and said "That reminds me…." She put down her fishing pole, stood up, and walked over to where I was sitting. She stepped over me, straddled my lap, and sat down. Wrapping her arms around me, she pulled my face to hers and kissed me with a fierceness of need and longing that we both shared. It was as if all the emotion we had shared in our dreams were released in this moment.

Somehow we wound up naked and covered in mud. I vaguely remember a frantic struggle to remove each other's clothing. Strangely, I could feel her emotion and thoughts in my head and hear my own thoughts mirrored in hers. The raw need and intense intimacy was almost more than I could handle, but there was no way to stop. We were on a runaway train of the sexual kind that would only stop when it ran off the cliff into an abyss of completion.

Exhausted and gasping for breath, we eventually wound up in the water. We nearly drowned ourselves before we finally gave in, put our clothes back on and cleaned up.

We were just gathering up our gear when we heard the girls come running down the path to their mother. We looked at each other and I said, "Just in the nick of time." She laughed and said, "I might just have to go to the old house. Check it out to make sure everything functions properly and keep tabs on my new tenant and…. collect the rent," she giggled and jogged to meet the girls running down the path.

3 YOU ARE SO BUSTED!

Maddey and Adey modeled all their new fashions. It was amazing. This morning they looked like little girls. This afternoon they looked like young teenagers. I had to admit I had been holding them back. I wanted them to be my little girls forever. They were growing into young women and somehow I almost missed it.

I heard the maturity creeping into their voices for some time now. I attributed it to the nature of their being the Balance. They often made mature cryptic comments and observations even before they could speak verbally, so I was used to those kinds of changes. Somehow I had missed the signs they were physically maturing as well. Thinking about them growing up and leaving for good when they became adults brought tears to my eyes. I made a silent vow to myself that I wouldn't miss another minute with them again if it killed me.

My girls were the Balance of all magic in the world, light and dark, good and bad. Without them there would be chaos and the earth would literally be ripped apart. There had always been a pair of a species born as the Balance since the dawn of time. They are not necessarily good or bad but simply without one you cannot have the other. Maddey is older by only 11 months, so they are not twins. One trait is equally as strong as the other child's. We believe they did not receive the power until both children were born. MaMere and I have talked about it many times. It was not apparent she was one half of the Balance until Adey was born. Neither child exhibited traits of good or bad, but simply one prefers sunlight and the other moonlight, ying and yang, light and dark.

In times when the pair that are the Balance were suppressed or separated from the other, there would be wars, pestilence and famine. Whichever child was being abused or controlled affected the general flow of magic that was normally attributed by lunar cycles or solar cycles. Humans, as well as supernatural creatures, would also experience changes and inconsistencies. Those that practice or worship, white or dark depending on the user, made using magic in those times extremely difficult and the results became unpredictable. Control was nearly impossible.

A group of people aligned with one type or the other determined whether good or evil reigned in the world. The Balance, a gift from God, is a pair usually born to parents who will protect and nurture them. Never would these parents harm them.

There have been times in history when they were captured or fell into the hands of people who used them to amplify their own powers and wishes for greed or personal gain. When this unfortunate event occurred, the pair would eventually be drained and die. Another pair would be born to new parents and the cycle would begin again.

It is for this reason we had been separated since the girls were babies. Never being able to do more than short visits and communicate telepathically drove me insane with the need to be with them sometimes. We were attacked by a Fae group called boggarts who were trying to capture me because of my bloodline. They had no idea my children were the Balance. Fortunately, they were completely inept and botched the whole kidnapping. It scares me to death even now to think if they had been successful in capturing me, as soon as they touched the children, they would have known the truth and the children would have been cruelly drained and left to die.

All that had now changed. It was only a matter of time before those who were looking for them would be able to put the pieces of the puzzle together (if they haven't already) and find them. With recent events, everyone now agreed it would be easier to defend all of them if they were together. The children were older now and not the defenseless babes they once were.

I thought to myself. I didn't give a damn what the consensus was. I was not leaving them again, no matter who got in my way. My mind made up, I turned my attention back to the girls.

We all giggled and oooed and aahhed over all their new trappings. Then the girls began showing me their new makeup kits. They turned to me in unison and informed me they needed a "make-over." I laughed and told them even if they were the mature beings of Balance on the inside they still inhabited the bodies of my young girls and there was a definite level of cosmetics that was acceptable for other young women of their age and appearance.

Grumbling about not being allowed to use everything in their kits, they finally settled down and were eager to begin their experimentations with cosmetics. I hadn't said no to anything but the stronger pigments and products for more experienced girls. With rapt attention, they absorbed all the techniques necessary to achieve a clean, wholesome, and well-groomed appearance. It helped that Aundrea was able to pull up videos of Hanna Montana and Selena Gomez for references.

Adey, who was never happy with anyone touching her long raven locks, even allowed her hair to be styled into a chignon. She could be heard grumbling at least it wouldn't slap her in the face when she was climbing trees.

I simply shook my head and put my head in my hands to hide my dismay and amusement and finally asked her, "If you don't like it so much, why are you doing it?" Adey shuffled her feet and lowered her head "Because I don't want to be left out and if Maddey is doing it then I need to do it too." I pulled her into a hug and told her, "You need to be your own person. Just because you are sisters doesn't mean that you will always be exactly alike. You might find that you would be happier sharing each other's differences just as much as what you both like together."

Adey sniffled slightly and said, "You mean if I think ruffles are scratchy and makeup feels like mud that burns my eyes, that I don't have to do it too?" I smiled and said, "That's right, besides I never liked that stuff when I was your age either. You may be more like me than you thought." Adey looked at me and gave me a rare, deeply dimpled smile and hugged me fiercely. Then she kicked off her new little sandals and ripped the hair out of the bun. She jumped right out of the window to run off into the swamp, happy to still be free to play.

Maddey watched the exchange silently. When her sister was gone, she watched me with an alarmed look. I noticed and said, "Just because ya'll are the Balance, does not mean y'all can't be individuals. I've been thinking about that for some time now. I believe if the two of you develop different strengths and personalities, you might be stronger and able to defend yourself better than any other pair that has come before." Maddey simply nodded in acknowledgement and turned back to the task of learning to look like a human teenager.

Stella, Aundrea, and Sam were among the gaggle of conspirators in make-over lessons. Sam, mysteriously quiet, sniffed and sampled every crème, powder, scent and fabric with great curiosity.

When Maddey was satisfied with her new appearance, Sam made her appearance. She had quietly disappeared somewhere toward the end of the make-over. She came into the bedroom dressed in a bridal gown turned inside out and the veil on backwards. She did her turn on our makeshift catwalk, then flopped down on the bed. She turned to me and pointing at the make-up kit she said happily, "My turn!" With wide eyes and shocked expressions, everyone was surprised that the young dragon would have any interest in human vanity products.

Stella asked Sam very carefully so as not to offend, "Where did ya get yo lovely new dress, Chere?" Sam beamed, obviously proud of herself, she told us while everyone was going from shop to shop getting things for the girls, she decided to do a little shopping of her own. She saw this pair of dolls in a store window wearing mating clothes. She explained that she had been watching humans for a long time and she had deduced that the sole purpose of their existence was to find a mate, make babies and die. Since she could now look like a human she had to make an effort to do all the things humans do and not arouse suspicion, so she bought the mating clothes, both outfits just to make sure she was prepared.

Aundrea, recovering from her shock a little quicker than the rest of us, asked her, "Are you saying you bought the male doll suit too?" Sam nodded vigorously, "Yes, when I asked for the mating suits the woman in the store thought I was mentally unbalanced and asked me if I had lost my guardian. I told her a few had applied for the position, but couldn't stand the heat. She didn't want to give them to me and told me if this wasn't a joke she needed to see proof I had the funds to purchase the clothing. I wasn't expecting that, so I left the store and went around to the back. I found some pebbles and rocks on the ground near an old coal burner with a few large chunks still in the bottom. I shifted my hand into my claw and applied pressure and heat to make the sparkly rocks everyone is always disturbing our caves for.

"When I came back in the store and asked her if they were enough or did she need more, she got really excited and told me that I could have the whole damned store if I wanted. By the way, we need to make arrangements to pick up all that stuff; here is the key to the front door."

Aundrea, again thinking quicker than

the rest of us, asked, "Just how big were these rocks?" Sam thought for a minute and said, "About the size of a bird's egg."

Aundrea turned around and leaned against the wall. She proceeded to bang her head on it. When she recovered, she looked at MaMere and said, "I will go call Joe and Hawk and let them know we have some damage control to do." She left the room to make her calls.

I blinked and turned back to Sam, "Ok, what type of look do you want to achieve?" Sam's eyes flashed green and slitted pupils blinked in for a moment, "I want to be ssssmooth and ssssssexy." I asked her where she had ever heard that before and why she wanted to be sexy. She told me she heard it on the television in the department store. She also told me she wanted to do what I did with Dan today with a human male of her choosing.

Stunned and embarrassed, I stammered and sputtered and told her I wasn't sure I understood what she meant, trying to ignore the question. Aundrea, being a dire wolf in her spirit form had excellent hearing. She came running back into the room, looked at Sam and then back at me. She realized what Sam was talking about and laughed. "That's why you have mud in your hair and all over the back of your pants! You are soooo busted! Spill it!"

At this point, Maddey, obviously tired of being a mature young woman, chose her timing perfectly to hide the fact she was missing her sister. She said she thought she heard Adey calling for her and exited out the same window, also minus her new shoes.

MaMere, Aundrea and Sam huddled around me, giggling and wanting details. I knew I wasn't going to get out of it, so I began to fess up.

MaMere, with the powers of the goddess Tethys, knew exactly what had happened, but she still sat and enjoyed the company and bonding with the rest of us.

Aundrea wanted details. "Was he good? Was he big or small?" She said, "You know, it's those quiet ones who don't feel the need to overcompensate for anatomical inadequacies, if you catch my drift. They also make the best lovers and are attentive and eager to please. Am I right, was he… attentive?" In answer to all her questions, I simply purred. I laughed and told her she was right on all counts. Feeling mischievous,

I told her he had been a swimmer and learned to hold his breath a really long time. Plus he has a great ass, too!

4 A PIRATE'S CRUISE

Jamie and her girls, along with most of the other females in attendance, encamped in Stella's room to try on and model all their new fashions. Time to do the "female thing." From the sounds of all the laughter and giggling, they appeared to be having a great time.

I was left to sit on the porch with one of Stella's impossibly old and rare books. I will never get over the immense treasure of literature that made up Stella's library.

I had been sitting there reading for some time when I heard Jean come lumbering up the steps. I really do like the guy, don't get me wrong, but I still get a little nervous when he comes up so quietly. I mean he *is* still a ferocious thirty foot alligator. His mouth is as big as the hood of a car. He always looks like he is smiling by the way his jaws curve up at the corners. You can't help but get the impression he is anticipating what you might taste like.

Jean Lafitte was MaMere's lover, boyfriend, and mate. He was actually the Pirate, Jean Lafitte. Yes, the same pirate that helped fight the British in the War of 1812.

Here is where I am going to confuse you, so let me clarify this. MaMere, or Estelle Eschte, Stella for short (her human alias) is actually Tethys, a titan of Greek history and the goddess of nurturing and motherhood, as well as the oceans, lakes and streams of the world. Anyway, she turned her lover, the infamous Pirate, Jean Lafitte, into an alligator to teach him to control his jealousy and temper when other males were in her vicinity.

My newly discovered abilities have allowed me to communicate with the old reptile and we have become good friends. If I had to admit it, he is about the closest friend I have really ever had. My difficulties with my eyesight limited my activities as a child. I never did become good at making friends or keeping them. I had acquaintances I worked with or saw on a daily basis, but no one I could actually say was a close friend.

He came up on the porch and lay length-wise (and still his tail was hanging off a bit) at my feet. He grunted and asked what my plans were now that I had gotten a job here in Louisiana.

I told him about the house Jamie offered to let me rent. He grunted and informed me it was right on the banks of Bayou LaSalle and he had been there once or twice. I asked him if it had been in his current form. He told me he had been an alligator long before Jamie was born. (Aha! A clue to her real age! Although from his research into her mother, Marie, she would have to be around 86 years old. She didn't look any older than 25.) He said he never really trusted Jamie's husband or any man associated with the females in his family. He would make periodic visits just to make sure they were doing ok.

I wondered to myself if Jamie knew how much Jean really cared about her. Jean asked me when I intended to make my move out here. I told him I would have to first get a ride into town and check out Jamie's house. Then I would probably hit the road for Los Angeles. I was dreading the trip out there and told him what I was thinking. He grinned, showing his teeth in his creepy gator way, and told me he might have an alternative - if I was game.

Curious at the tone of his thoughts, I asked him what he had in mind. He hesitated for a moment, then said it would be the experience of a lifetime if I was up to the task. Ok, now I was hooked. "What are you getting at?" He said he had been thinking about getting away for a long time, but never had the means to get very far in his altered state. I could understand what he meant, anyone around here seeing a thirty foot alligator out in open water would shoot him just for the trophy.

He told me that in order to make the trip I would have to do a lot of the work, but it would probably change my life forever. I laughed at that and said, "Any more than my life has been changed in the last three weeks? For instance, I am currently conversing with an alligator and legendary pirate from the 1800's telepathically! Not to mention all the other changes I have experienced since I got here."

He said, "You have a point Mon Amie. What I have in mind will change your spirit and test your mettle as a man." I leaned forward and replied, "Uh huhhhh. So. Basically what you're telling me is you need a break from this place and a designated driver?"

He grunted a couple of times in succession and popped his teeth at me as a physical response to my question. He told me telepathically to follow him and I would see what he meant. I returned the book I had been reading back to the shelf where I found it and followed him to the far side of the island, near the beach where we battled the trolls. He grunted once again as a physical signal to look closer at the jungle of trees and brush and then asked me telepathically what I thought. I looked at him like he was crazy. I didn't see what he wanted me to see.

He hissed at me in frustration and stomped into the brush where he started tugging at some of the vines growing in the trees.

As I looked closer at what he was trying to uncover, I realized what I thought were trees were actually the masts of a small ship, or schooner, if I had my terminology correct. Now enthusiastic, I started helping him pull the vegetation away. I realized it was a ship. It had been dry-docked here and skillfully camouflaged to keep it from being discovered. The more we cleared the vegetation away the more I realized it must have been here well before he became reptilian.

Once we had it uncovered, we stood back to look at it and take it all in. Sarcastically, I looked down at him and asked if he had other treasures hidden around here. He only blinked at me and continued to admire his ship. I noticed it was named the Witch's Bane. I asked him what it meant. He laughed and told me when he came to Barataria, this was one of his fastest ships. He used it regularly to get into a small cove quickly to load or unload cargo without being seen and in fairly shallow water. He said he escaped from the British many times during the Battle of New Orleans and it was one of the few ships he didn't have to buy back once Claiborne, then governor of Louisiana, seized all his assets even after President Madison gave him a full pardon for his help during the war. He actually growled and thrashed his tail, nearly knocking me over remembering the slights of his past.

I could tell this still irritated him quite a bit, even after all this time. He said he had only one regret. It was not being able to see Claiborne's face when the bounty posters were put up. I asked him what he meant and he laughed. He said the pompous bastard put a bounty on his head offering five hundred dollars for anyone that would bring him in. He retaliated by posting his own bounty on Claiborne for fifteen hundred dollars to anyone who delivered Governor Claiborne to Barataria. They were signed, *Jean Laffite*.

I asked him why was the name Witch's Bane on his ship. He said originally, he had named it the Sea Nymph, but because he was on the Sea Nymph so much, Stella became jealous of her and told him she would never step foot on the little ship. So he renamed it

Witch's Bane just to tease her.

(It was a little odd for me to imagine Stella as being the jealous one.) Treading cautiously and steering the conversation into another direction, I told him it still looked like it was in good condition. He grunted in approval and said the gnomes were mostly responsible. It was their job to maintain the island in return for Stella's hospitality. The fact that the ship was on the island, it was also maintained to a certain degree. They were the ones who pulled it out of the water and put it up on pilings for dry docking. Even after the war, he still had his men to feed. So he made use of it until he was unable to sail any longer. He said they also made periodic repairs to keep her in exactly the same condition they found her in. I asked if Stella knew about it. He grunted at me and said "Of course she knows, she's a goddess and this is her island. Let's just say she kept it here because it is mine."

Blunt as always, I came right out and asked him. "Do you still love her?" He sighed and said, "Yes, I still love Stella. But I yearn for the open waters and freedom as well. I want to experience it just one more time before I give in to the inevitability that Stella will never change me back to a human again." I told him so far, when she talked about him, it was obvious the feeling was mutual. He said, "Yes, but a goddess also means sometimes it is easy to forget what the passing of time means to those who face their own mortality and eventual death. To her, it was if it all happened only last month instead of one hundred and ninety five years, three months, and two days ago."

If he had a watch, he would probably be able to pin it down to the minute. What do you say to something like that? Oh, she'll get over it when she calms down? As sad as it is, the old alligator was right. It brought home the point if you pissed someone off with these kinds of powers, you wouldn't just serve a little time in jail for your indiscretion. You might find yourself serving out your sentence for all eternity. I would definitely be watching what I said more closely from now on.

Standing in thought for a while, looking at the ship, I sort of felt a little sorry for the guy. Making a theatrical gesture with arms wide open I announced, "What the hell! I've got plenty of time on my hands right now. I would have to be a complete imbecile to pass up the chance to sail on the open seas in an actual pirate ship with the infamous pirate Jean Lafitte!"

His tail began whipping. I could tell he was excited I had accepted his offer. We both looked back on the ship, beginning to feel the excitement of adventure. Then I noticed something and said, "We might have a slight problem, Captain." He responded, "What's that?" I couldn't believe he had overlooked the obvious. I said, "How are we going to get it into the water? I am assuming you do not want Stella to know, nor do I think she will help you get the very ship she has always hated back in the water and escape this place, even for a little while. Even if we do get it in the water, how are you gonna get on the ship?"

He laughed and said, "You leave the details to me, Mon Amis. I have had plenty of time to work it all out. I have been feeding the gnomes a little lagniappe for quite some time now and they owe me a favor or two. But you are right about one thing. I don't want Stella to know. She probably already does. I just don't want to have to talk to her about it if I can help it."

5 A QUEEN AWAKENS

Broken and bloody, Brady Bauchan literally dragged himself back to Crowley's office. Empty and eerily silent, he sank into Crowley's chair. Most of his clan was dead or wounded. The dragons and that huge wolf had cleaned his clock. His right leg was broken and his back and left arm shredded from his escape from the dragon's claws.

He would be dead right now if it hadn't been for the fact that two of his trolls distracted the dragon long enough for him to get away. He almost made it when a wolf, bigger than any other he ever heard of, grabbed him by the leg and shook him like a puppy with a new chew toy. It flung him to the ground where he bashed his head on a rock and was knocked unconscious.

He supposed he should be dead. More bodies were piled on top of him while he lay there. He was scooped up along with the carcasses and loaded onto a shrimp boat for disposal. He had come to on the deck of the boat, then waited for the opportunity to slip over the side while the Cajuns were cleaning the carcasses for bait meat.

As he watched, he recognized one of the carcasses they were working on... his dead brother. They were picking his bones clean. He vowed not only would that old Swamp Bitch pay, he also owed a debt of revenge to all who her kill what was left of his family before this all started.

When the vampires and trolls started taking the house apart, they almost had her and he could taste victory. He couldn't believe she found a way to save herself. He conceded they underestimated the depth of the old woman's powers and the loyalty of those who helped her.

He would rebuild the army. He would even work with that stuck-up, condescending vampire if he had to, but he *would* get his revenge. He would see that old woman stripped of her flesh for fish-bait just like his brother; only he wouldn't be working on a dead corpse when he did it.

He began rifling through Crowley's desk, looking for anything that might be of use to him. Literally tearing the desk apart, he discovered a hidden drawer in the back. In it was a remote control that looked strangely similar to a garage door opener.

He clicked the button and a panel behind the desk slid to the side. It revealed a short hallway with three doors, one door on each side and one at the end of the hall. His leg roughly splinted, he limped to the first door and found it locked. Cursing and growling in frustration, he was too weak to break the door down. He went back to Crowley's desk and searched for keys.

Suddenly a phone rang on Crowley's

desk. He picked it up and nearly had a heart attack. He recognized the woman's voice on the other end.

"Brady Bauchan, you have disobeyed me."

Brady stuttered, "Yes, uh no Queen Mab...we thought you still in your slumber, I...it has been a long time since you have wakened. I was going to...."

"Come to the mound immediately, I have decided to give you a chance to redeem yourself."

"Queen Mab, I am wounded." Immediately he felt intense, crushing, burning pain shooting up his leg and through his body to all his extremities. He was healed of all his wounds.

"Do not whine and don't dawdle. Do you think my time worthless?"

Brady was now shaking violently with pain and fear. There was no escape from her. He started to reply and realized that the line was dead. He rose from the chair he collapsed in and realized he actually soiled his clothes during his "healing" when the phone rang again. He picked it up immediately. "Bring the vampire with you. The keys are in a false book on the shelf." The line was again silent with the finality of her command.

Wondering how she knew exactly what he was doing, he looked around for hidden cameras. Seeing none, he went to the bookshelves and started opening the books. He threw them on the floor in his frantic search for the keys. He knew she was going to get even madder with every second he wasted doing as she commanded.

Finally finding the keys in the last book on the bottom shelf, he ran to the first door and unlocked it to find a bedroom lavishly furnished with a canopy bed and decadent trappings. He grumbled. It figured that Crowley, the pompous ass, would have to have a bedroom only a porn star would covet.

Seeing a large armoire of clothing, he quickly stripped himself of his soiled and ruined clothing. He grabbed a shirt and started to put it on. He realized it had the stylized cuffs and tailored cut Crowley was so fond of and threw it on the floor. He looked a little harder and found the one pair of jeans Crowley had and put them on. Though they were a little long, he preferred them to the others, eschewing all the other leather trappings and designer frippery the man usually favored. Anything to get out of the embarrassing mess he had just been wearing.

He left the room to open the other door across the hall. He inserted the first key and opened the door only to find a door to a steel bank-grade vault. This must be where Crowley had all his valuables. He would have to come back later with some specialized equipment and get into it even if he had to blow the whole damn building up. He felt his spirits lift at the prospect of what might be in that vault.

He all but ran to the last door in his haste to not keep the queen waiting. His hands were shaking so hard he almost couldn't get the key in the lock. It was an empty room with only a massive stone coffin. This has to be the vampire's ...bed? He tried to push the lid off the coffin, but it wouldn't budge. Frustrated beyond belief he began cursing again. He looked around for something he could pry it off with and finding nothing, he leaned against it and began to think. As he did, he rapped his knuckles on the lid a few times and the lid began to pivot to one side, revealing the vampire inside.

Smiling, the man sat up and said,

"All you had to do was knock; manners are everything, my man. Come now, we mustn't keep the lady waiting."

Brady, realizing the vampire knew he had been looking for him all along, fumed with indignation. Just when he thought with Crowley gone, he would finally be in control. He knew that he was no match for this creature and would once again be relegated back to being the lackey. When this was over, the vampire had to go. That is... IF he survived his encounter with Queen Mab.

6 THELMA AND LOUISE IN NOLA

Phone calls were made to Joe and Hawk to find the shopkeeper of the bridal store Sam had apparently purchased. Joe called back and said he found the woman at the bank. He managed to stop her before she completely withdrew all of her savings to go shopping. She thought she would use the stones as collateral for some sizeable loans. He had to do quite a bit of fast talking to get her to relinquish the stones. He finally told her if she insisted on keeping them she would be arrested for receiving stolen property, hindering a police investigation and tampering with evidence.

He assured her she would be compensated as a victim of a crime. She would retain her store and receive several thousand dollars for the wedding ensemble the young female thief took, plus the time lost when the shop was closed. She still wasn't happy, but she turned them over. He grumped she should be grateful since she had made more for her afternoon of inconvenience than the store earned in the past five years.

Aundrea told him to quit whining. It was about to get worse. She was going to take Sam to New Orleans for a weekend of beauty and shopping. Sam was on her way to get some of her things for their trip and meet her back in Dulac in thirty minutes.

He asked, "What kind of things does a dragon-girl need anyway?"

Aundrea, thinking that was a very good question, said, "How would I know? Her new mating clothes? Or maybe dragon panties? You know. The kind that mold to your body and are fire retardant in case you get really hot and bothered?"

Joe groaned and begged her to please stay out of trouble. There were only so many strings he could pull. With what happened during their attack, those strings were unraveling fast.

Right on time, Sam came gliding in and landed right next to her, changing into human form once again.

"Where's Max?" Aundrea asked her, hanging up on Joe.

Sam said, "He had other plans," then grumbled something about going fishing.

Aundrea said, "I thought you guys just gobbled up whatever came close. I didn't know you preferred seafood."

Sam grumbled again, "We don't."

By the look on her face, Aundrea decided to let that one go. She handed her a pretty little sundress, sandals and floppy to wear. Sam was ecstatic. Once dressed, they got into Aundrea's convertible and embarked on their road trip.

Having checked into a little hotel right off Bourbon Street, Aundrea asked Sam if she brought anything of value they could trade for cash. Sam's jaws enlarged and she literally coughed up several large diamonds, emeralds and even a couple of large gold boulders (too big to be called a nugget).

Aundrea's eyes popped at the treasure Sam produced and asked if there were any way she could trim them down a bit. Sam looked at her curiously and asked, "Why? In my observations, humans were happier with the concept of the bigger, the better."

Aundrea laughed and said, "You are probably right, but we might have a little trouble converting such large gems without attracting the attention of the authorities. Besides, we can go shopping sooner if we can trade them for cash faster."

At that, Sam readily complied, morphing one hand to her dragon's claw and crushing the jewels into smaller, more manageable stones. Aundrea was amazed Sam could transform only a specific part of her body. She would love to be able to have that kind of control over her own wolf form. Aundrea, approving size and shape, told her their first stop would be at a brokerage that specialized in buying and selling raw, uncut gems.

When they arrived at the jewelry

brokerage, they were ushered into a small office. Aundrea was greeted with apparent familiarity. Though Sam always appeared to be unobservant, she rarely missed anything. She raised an eyebrow in question to Aundrea.

Aundrea explained, with a guilty look and more than a little evasiveness, that yes, she had been here a couple of times before. She just happened to acquire items of value from time to time through her enemies and other odd jobs. She said, "I just think of it as the spoils of war." That was a term Sam was familiar with. She was satisfied with the explanation.

When the gentleman asked Aundrea what had she brought this time, she poured the jewels from her purse into a heaping pile on his little velvet-lined tray.

The man's eyes bugged out. He said, "As always, do I have your assurance these items are not stolen and you are the sole owner?"

Aundrea just laughed and said, "You should know better than that. Have I ever brought anything with questionable origin to you before? Besides, don't you always make me sign affidavits attesting my ownership?"

Ever wary, the man told her he would only be able to give her a portion of the value of the gems until they could be authenticated. She nodded in consent while he began inspecting the stones.

As he viewed one, then another, he became more and more excited. He said he rarely saw gems with so much color and clarity in this size. The diamonds appeared to be flawless. The gold was 24 karats; extremely rare in raw form. He asked, "Do you have some sort of mining operation or have you discovered how to make the jewels yourself?"

Sam started to answer and Aundrea stomped her foot hard. "Owww! That hurt!" Aundrea took advantage of the distraction and said, "Silly, he is just joking, of course! Can you imagine what would happen if someone found a way to make their own diamonds and other precious jewels? Why, it would destroy the entire world economy and free trade as we know it."

The man, obviously sensing the conversation was getting touchy said, "Based on my initial analysis and the amount of cash we have on hand at the moment, I can only give you about a quarter of the value of these gems. We will forward the rest to your account, as usual, within the week."

Aundrea consented to the arrangements and said, "Just wire the money to my account. I will be using my debit card this weekend. How much is the first transaction so I won't over spend?"

He replied, "That will be two million dollars. I don't think even you can spend that much in that short a time unless you gave it away. You should see it in your account within the hour. The remaining six million will be available by the end of the week. The stones would be worth ten million dollars but are raw and uncut. Therefore it reduces the value somewhat. Is this acceptable to you?"

Aundrea tried to hide her shock and had trouble finding her voice. "Yes, that will be fine. It was a pleasure doing business with you, as usual."

Sam was investigating the Newton's Cradle on a table by the window, clicking and holding the balls as they clacked against each other. Aundrea grabbed her by the hand and practically dragged her out of the office. When they got outside, Aundrea leaned against the building chanting,

"Ohmygodohmygodohmygod, OH, MY GOD!" She grabbed Sam by the shoulders and began hopping and dancing around and around, "We're rich!"

Sam laughed and said "If it makes you this happy, I can bring you more if you like."

Aundrea calmed down a bit and said, "I'm gonna take you shopping and I appreciate your gift. I'm gonna kick myself later for telling you this, but you should probably try to set up your own accounts so you can support yourself when you are in human form. I am going to make an appointment with Hawk's solicitors for you so he can advise you to make the necessary investments. This will protect you in the event of some kind of disaster. These guys have been working with us "supers" for some time now. Without their advice, many of us would have had to resort to losing everything we have every hundred years or so just to keep from being discovered as something other than human."

Sam, although ignorant of modern terminology, was no idiot. She understood immediately the importance of not having to start all over again. To have a sense of permanence in her life was something she and Max had always longed for. For that alone, she vowed she would be eternally grateful to this woman. Maybe this era of humanity would be worth sticking around for.

Sam laughed with Aundrea for a little while longer and said, "Can we get something to eat now?"

Aundrea laughed and replied, "Anything you want, sister. I feel like I could eat the north end out of a south bound elephant right now."

Sam said, "Yeah, that's a lot of meat, mmmm…. I didn't think they had elephants in North America. Where do they keep them?"

Aundrea stared at her a moment then reminded herself she might also have to give Sam a lesson in humor and sarcasm.

After consuming every item on the menu at Brennan's and driving the cooks and wait staff to the point of exhaustion (only large tips kept them from being thrown out), they were finally ready to do some shopping. Aundrea told her they were going to start with a spa and get pampered before they got pretty just to get in the right frame of mind. She told Sam the whole purpose was to relax and let the stress of the day-to-day world drift away.

They were in the sauna relaxing with their eyes closed after their massages when an attendant came in to deliver towels and ice water. She started screaming bloody murder. Aundrea jumped up and realized Sam had relaxed a little too much. Most of her human form was now Dragon.

When the manager came in to see what the woman was screaming about, the only thing she saw were two women melting their stress away. Apologizing profusely for disturbing their spa experience, the manager ushered the attendant away, muttering something about too much caffeine and keeping VIP guests happy - she didn't care if they had two heads. As soon as they left, Sam looked at Aundrea a little sheepishly and said, "Sorry…. I got lost in the moment?"

Aundrea nearly doubled over laughing and told her not to worry about it. She started changing to her wolf when she hit puberty and had a hard time maintaining forms, too. Sam relaxed again, finding another thing she had never had before… a friend.

7 GETTING SHIP SHAPE

The next morning I heard Jean calling for me in my head at just about sunrise. I rolled off my bunk and slipped some pants on and stumbled into the kitchen. Stella was sitting at the little table drinking coffee and working with some herbs in a basket.

"Mornin Chere," she said. "Good Morning," I replied, accepting the cup of coffee she handed me. "You're up early dis morning, yeah." "Uh, yeah, uh, I uhhh, told Jean I would go for a swim

with him today. I had no idea he meant
at dawn," I answered, still too sleepy to
be able to think of a better way to evade
her question. She chuckled, "Yeah, he
never was known for his patience, non.
You have been a good friend to him,
Dan. He's been needin someone lahke
you for a long tahm."

I told her that he was a good guy
and I liked him a lot too. I took a sip of
the strong brew that was called coffee
here in Louisiana. No wonder the
Cajuns were always up running around
doing something. You rarely saw them
sit still. How could you, with this stuff in
your system? When I first tried it, I
thought it was going to take the flesh off
my esophagus, it was so strong.
Becoming more accustomed to it now, I
have come to appreciate the richness of
the flavor and welcome the instant jolt
of alertness it provided me.

When I was living in California my
habits were mostly nocturnal; sleeping
during the brightest part of the day,
rising in late afternoon wearing
extremely dark sunglasses so that I
would still have access to businesses
that closed in the evenings. Journalism
as a profession worked well for me being
able to set my own hours.

Getting accustomed to this new schedule of rising with the sun and working to sundown was an easier adjustment than I thought. The Cajun culture is a joyous one. They celebrated life every day with large families that lived together, worked together and raised their children together. Money, wealth or social status made no difference in these families. At the end of the day or week they all joined together, contributing equally for a meal and a reunion of family ties and friendships.

They never meet a stranger, there were no "hey you's" here, instead it was customary to address someone as "friend or Chere" in place of a name if you had never met. I had asked Joe about this once and he told me that laziness, drunks, drugs and those that harmed others were not tolerated. If the law didn't take care of them, they were shunned from the community and forced to leave or make their own way alone or with the other dregs of society. Parents played an important role in the raising of their children, setting examples by having them take an active part in family businesses like shrimping, hunting or whatever they did to earn a living. It was said that Cajun children only got into trouble on dad's day off. The rest of the time they were too tired.

He said that they lived the life God intended, enjoying every minute with love in your heart for your fellow man. Sure, everyone had bad times and dark days, but in the end, you could always count on someone in your family for help when you needed it.

Stella was strangely quiet while I sipped my coffee, seemingly engrossed in her task of sorting and mincing her herbs. It didn't escape my attention that she didn't ask where I was going with Jean or what we were going to do. I had a feeling she knew and was giving me the respect of not putting me on the spot and having to out my new friend. I finished my coffee and told her that I had probably better not keep him waiting. She just nodded as I left the kitchen.

Jean was indeed waiting for me on the beach, grunting again and pacing in irritation at having to wait so long for me. As I got closer, I noticed that he had somehow dug a deep trench from the shoreline to the sailboat and a little ways underneath it. Amazed at his progress, I asked how he had done it.

He told me that he wasn't a lazy bones sleeping all night. He hurried me along telling me that there was still a lot of work to be done before the tide came in again tonight.

Tonight! I hadn't expected to leave that soon. Hearing my panic, he told me don't get your pantaloons in a twist. We are simply going to get it in the water to test for leaks and make sure it was ship shape for our trip. "Oh, ok." I said, somewhat relieved that I still had time to tell Jamie that I was leaving and maybe be able to spend a little more time with her. I was still trying to figure out how I was going to do that without ratting Jean out. As soon as Jamie figured it out, she would go straight to Stella. I was sure of it.

We worked all day digging the trench deeper and clearing away the undergrowth. At about noon, I knew that we might have a problem. I asked Jean how he was going to get onboard once it was in the water. He said again that he had already thought of that and he made me get up on the deck and check the block and tackle that secured a small dinghy.

Surprisingly, everything seemed to still be in good working order. I asked him how this was possible and he told me to remember that the gnomes were responsible for maintaining everything on this island, including keeping things from deteriorating. They took their jobs seriously.

He told me that there should be two "L" shaped braces that fit into reinforced notches on the deck near the railing at the stern. Finding them, I inserted them into the notches as he instructed. He showed me how to rig the pulleys to the braces to a platform he had dragged up and I began to see what his plan was. However, I doubted that these would be strong enough to lift him. He was a lot bigger and heavier than the small dinghy. Even with the ropes and pulleys, I didn't know if I would have the strength to hoist him up. He told me to have faith and I would find the strength I needed when the time came.

Our next problem came later in the afternoon. The trench, finally dug to Jean's satisfaction, was a feat in itself. I shoveled and he wallowed. He used his body like a bobcat. Sweeping sand and mud with his tail and at times, using his massive mouth like a front-end loader to excavate under the boat. Exhausted by that time, I was catching my breath near the trench and looked up toward the masts. Wondering what it would look like to see the sails billow in the wind, I asked Jean where the sails were.

Still working and mumbling something about weak landlubbers, he said without looking up, "Are you daft? They are tied to the masts, Mon Amie." I looked at the masts and all around the ship, "No they're not." Finally he turned and sarcastically began lecturing me on what a sail was when he saw that they were indeed gone. "Sacre bleu! They were there last night." We both stood there just staring when I noticed a movement on a large rock off in the trees and a flash of orange, black and white, it suddenly dawned on me what had happened to the sails. Jean, too busy cursing and popping his jaws and slapping the ground with his tail didn't even notice that I had walked away from him.

Scratchy Patchy, or Bernice in her human form, was sitting on the rock grooming herself. I walked up to her and sat down. She began to rub her little weird cat body back and forth on my arm and bumping me with her head, wanting petting. I talked to her calmly and slowly about the sailboat and how we were getting it all cleaned up for a trip. She stopped her pleas for attention and sat down looking at me with her one cat eye and one human eye as if she was quite upset with what I was doing. I told her that we would be going to California to get my things so that I could come back and live here. She got up and bumped her little head against me and looked at me with questioning in her eyes. Yes, I told her, I am going to be living here from now on, but I have to go collect my things. She stood up on her hind legs and put her little paws on my chest and began licking my chin with her little raspy tongue. I petted her a minute longer and asked her if she knew what happened to the sails. She looked me right in the eye and jumped down off the boulder and gave that little hop and tail twitch that meant "follow me" that she always does and took off deeper into the trees.

A good ways in, she brought me to a pile of leaves and brush and grabbed something and began batting at it with her paw. Looking closer, I found the sails, the anchor, several coils of rope and a myriad of other things she had absconded with. I patted her little head, scratched her behind the ears and said,

"Thank you," and told her that I would have to bring her something pretty back when I returned from my trip.

I guess Jean had recovered from his tantrum and noticed that I was gone. I heard him calling for me and I answered him. In a minute he came lumbering up and saw what I had found. As soon as the little calico cat saw Jean she hissed and spit at him and took off back into the brush.

Jean looked at me and said, "Don't tell me, she didn't want you to leave so she hid our tackle." "Yup, you got it." He snorted and popped his jaws, "If she wasn't so pitiful looking and loyal to Stella, I would have eaten her a long time ago." I asked him, "I take it that this isn't the first time that she has done something like this?" "I have brought Stella things, presents and tokens and left them for her only to find out the damn cat had stolen them. She does seem to like you though. I don't know how much treasure she has stolen from me over the years and I've never been able to get her to give back so much as an earring."

I helped get all the gear back on the deck. With Jean dragging the anchor behind him and me carrying the sails, it took us a good two hours. How the little cat got them down and pulled so far out here was a mystery. I was pooped, so I told him that I was going to call it a day. I had some other things that I needed to take care of before we left. He grunted and told me that he would see me bright and early in the morning. There was nothing bright about his idea of morning.

Freshly showered, I met Jamie on the beach side of the little island. We walked along the beach that evening watching the sunset and truly happy to just be together. We talked about her girls, the house, what our shared interests were. I asked her if she would get bored with me like she did her first husband. She said, "I dunno, you gonna expect me to clean house and watch football every night?" She was funny and made me laugh.

There was no awkwardness between us. It was as if I had found a long lost friend and we were catching up. It was full dark and the moon had risen when the subject was steered to talking about getting my things and the move back here, when I decided it was time I broke the news to her that I was going to leave in a few days for California to get my things. I had already made the call to my landlord letting him know the situation.

Jamie smiled and told me that the girls were really having fun with MaMere, Sam and Aundrea right now and probably wouldn't miss her for a few days, so it wouldn't be a problem for her to get away now. If we planned it right, we could fly down one morning, hire a moving company to pack up all my things and then arrange to have them shipped back here and only be gone for a weekend at most. After we made all our arrangements, we could spend the rest of the weekend together alone. She waggled her eyebrows and grinned mischievously.

Uh, oh... she thought I was asking her to go with me. I realized that I was in a pickle. I couldn't tell her that this was a guy thing and that I didn't want her to go because she would know that Jean was leaving the island with me.

At my hesitation and lack of enthusiasm for her plans she began to search my mind. I felt her probing and quickly put up a wall to block her as Stella had taught me only a few days ago. Stella explained to me that my newfound empathic abilities would make it easy for me to eavesdrop in other people's heads, but that I needed to be careful, because it would also give them a direct link to what was in my own head.

Jamie obviously jumped to the wrong conclusion when she felt the wall go up because she stopped walking, turned to me and slapped the daylights out of me.

"Oh, that's the way it's gonna be huh? You got what you wanted and now you're done? You little rat bastard! I ought to castrate you right here and now just to teach you a lesson!"

She reached for her knife at her hip and realized that she wasn't wearing it and she took a breath and started yelling at me again, "You know what? You're not worth it! Don't worry; you don't have to sleep with the landlady just to make sure you get the lease! In fact, you don't ever have to see me again!" Then she ran off back the way we had come.

I didn't know what to say to her; she never gave me a chance. I tried to reach out to her with my mind, but all I got was a raging scream in my brain. She had misunderstood completely. I felt like killing Jean for getting me into this mess. She was really going to try to castrate me!

8 TRUTHS AND CONSEQUENCES

Aundrea and Sam, exhausted from their whirlwind shopping trip, arrived at Hawk's. Aundrea watched her adopted aunt and uncle and relaxed into the routine of what was now home to her.

Hawk's wife, Lynne, never turned anyone away. Their home was large enough to house an army and Lynne enjoyed every minute of it. She loved the hustle and bustle of a busy household and ran a tight and orderly ship. There was always something good to eat on the stove or in the refrigerator. She and Hawk had three sons and one daughter. Though Hawk, Jace and Jada had birds as spirit totems or were-beasts, they certainly didn't eat like birds.

Lynne, unique in that she had more than one Were animal, was also a bird and a fox. Both of those species were not big eaters but they needed to be fed constantly. Hence the reason Lynne was always cooking or preparing something to eat in her oversized kitchen.

She always laughed sarcastically when Hawk would brag about sparing no expense to make sure she had whatever she needed. She would "clarify" to whoever was listening that it was just because he wanted to make sure she never had an excuse not to whip up whatever he was hungry for, his being a bottomless pit and all. Hawk never took offense and would lean down and snuggle her closely and say that not everything he was hungry for was prepared in a kitchen, but it could be arranged if that's what she preferred. Blushing furiously, she would slap him on the shoulder and tell him that if he didn't stop teasing her she would go on a cooking strike and see where that got him.

With his predatory eyes narrowed at her pretend threat, he would respond, "I can still hunt and I prefer my meat rare anyway." She responded, mocking him that he couldn't fly if he was tied to the bed.

Their children were adults now, some with children of their own and Hawk and Lynne still loved each other and played like newlyweds.

Hawk and Lynne had restored the old antebellum plantation home situation on the banks of the lazy Bayou Black in Houma, Louisiana. Lynne told him when they first met that she had always thought that the old abandoned place was beautiful to her. She had played there as a child and hidden in it several times to escape being beaten by her pack for being different.

For a wedding present, Hawk had presented her with the deed to the property. Together, they worked restoring the place to its original glory, right down to the finest detail. The old slave quarters were converted to bunk houses and a safe haven for anyone who needed it. The house itself had twelve bedrooms. Beautiful gardens were tended by Lynne herself. She had a thriving horticulture business that specialized in hybridizations and rare finds. In this, she worked closely with MaMere for some of those exceptional novelties.

There was only one new addition to the property from the original design. It was a fully functioning laboratory facility accessed by one outside loading dock door and then a door from their bedroom. Hawk wanted to make certain no one just wandered in. When he started working out the architectural plans, she told him that it would be fine, but there had to be an atrium that they could use to be together so he wouldn't bury himself in his work and forget that she was there for fifteen or twenty years. You might think this strange, but Hawk can get very focused on his research and they both have a very long lifespan, so that was a very valid fear for her.

Aundrea and Sam plopped down at the large island in the middle of the kitchen and began nibbling on the platters of food that Lynne had prepared. As soon as Sam had Lynne's attention, she stuck out her hands and shouted, "Look, I got my claws sharpened! Aren't they pretty!" Aundrea looked at Lynne and explained, "I had to pull her aside for a few minutes before the mani /pedi and make sure she kept the nails in human form so she wouldn't freak out the nail tech."

"Good thinking," Lynne whispered to Aundrea before she turned back to Sam and said, "Wow, they look great with so many colors. Not the normal boring kind that all match, like so many other girls get."

Sam, obviously vindicated by something Aundrea must have said about her choices stuck out her tongue said, "See, I told you so. Why settle for just one color when you can have them all!" She scooped up a whole platter of food for herself and went to eat it at the table without interruption.

Lynne looked at Aundrea and told her not to criticize too much; she needed to remember the time when she went shoe shopping for the first time with her own money and she chewed one of every shoe so that she had an excuse to wear them all for the first time faster.

Aundrea put her head in her hands and said, "Yeah, I remember, but I was twelve and eager to show Miss Snotty

Britches at school that I had just as many shoes as she did. Some of them were even too small and really hurt my feet, but they were on sale and I figured the more, the better. Then I overheard her laughing at me with her friends and making up nasty nicknames."

Lynne casually asked her, "Speaking of freaking people out, that's not the same girl that you took into the swamp during the wolves' full moon pack hunt at the summer solstice celebration, is it?" Aundrea just giggled evilly.

Lynne told her that she heard from a friend that the poor girl is still in therapy and still has to be sedated during the full moon and hides in her closet when she hears a dog barking. Aundrea, only a little chastised, grumbled, "She won't be so quick to make fun of people who are different anymore."

Lynne continued to prepare the dinner and putter around her kitchen as she talked, seemingly too busy to watch Aundrea's pride inflate, she went on, "If I remember right, that was also the first time you were able to change forms fully without help from MaMere or Jamie." Aundrea, now even prouder of her accomplishments grinned even bigger than before.

Shoving a large casserole pan into the oven Lynne went on, "Yes, you were able to change into not only a wolf, but you channeled the great prehistoric dire wolf spirit totem of the old shaman that had been helping us with your changes. Even as a child, your wolf was bigger and stronger than any wolf before you." Aundrea, now beginning to glow in Lynne's praise raised her chin and held her head high.

Lynne asked her if she remembered what happened to that nice old man who had helped their family so much. Aundrea was thoughtful for a moment and said that she figured that he had just gone back into the woods where he came from when their family didn't need him anymore, now that Jamie and MaMere were able to help the other children survive their first changes.

Lynne shook her head and said, "You really don't remember, do you?" Aundrea looked at her blankly and Lynne continued, "You ate him. You ate that kind old man because you were crazed with the pain of the change and so full of vengeance and anger at that little girl, you couldn't focus on anything else. When you completed your change and went after the girl, the old man was the only wolf fast enough to reach you in time to stop you from killing her."

"That little girl watched you change. She was horrified and ran for her life from you and then watched in complete terror. She watched as the old man that she had seen in the drugstore just that same morning and who had offered her a piece of candy, change. She watched him battle you to the death. You were eating him while he was still alive when we found you. It took the entire pack to pull you away and restrain you. The alpha wanted to kill you for going rogue, but with his last breath, the old man begged us to save your life, for you were rare and he said he was old and ready for his death and that in time that you could learn to control your rage."

Aundrea's eyes were swimming with tears, "That's why the other wolves shun me. I thought it was jealousy because I am the strongest. I'm as bad as that old gator of MaMere's!"

Lynne made her look her in the eyes and said, "Do you still think that the punishment you sought fit the crime? How about your crime? Do you even remember her name?" Aundrea blinked and nodded, "Brittney, Brittney...Chamont?" Lynn said,

"Chauvin, her name is Brittney Chauvin and our family has paid for all that girl's medical bills over the years, anonymously, all this time. Maybe it's time you took over that responsibility, hmmm?"

Aundrea, stunned and humiliated at the revelation, put her head down and agreed with a nod of her head. Lynne told her that she could get all the particulars from Hawk after dinner.

Sam watched and listened to the entire exchange without comment. After dinner Aundrea slipped off to change and run her humiliation off down the bayou. Sam watched her go and slipped off quietly as well. When Aundrea had tired herself out, she changed back to human and climbed in the branches of an old oak dripping with Spanish moss and began crying.

Sam had watched her friend from the air and when the tears were mostly spent, she landed on the tree and changed back to human form and hugged her friend. They sat there quietly for such a long time when Aundrea got up, announced that her butt hurt and that she had some paperwork to take care of. She thanked Sam and asked her if she needed a ride. Sam said she was good and jumped in the air, changing to her dragon, and flew away.

Aundrea watched the great beast, now her best friend, fly across the moon and vowed to herself that she couldn't change what she had done, but she could teach Sam not to make the same mistakes she had. With Sam's temperament and power, it wasn't going to be like corking a volcano. Aunt Lynne was a very wise woman.

9 WATER, WATER EVERYWHERE AND NARY A DROP TO DRINK

Jean called to me in my thoughts. He was insistent that I come to the ship with all my things immediately. Grumbling to myself that it was still dark outside, I threw my clothes on and gathered my belongings, stuffing them into my suitcase and ran for the front door. When I stepped out onto the old porch, Stella was sitting in her chair waiting for me. She got up, handed me a large duffle bag and a thermos of coffee.

"Dat's de provisions dat ya will need fo ya trip, Chere. Dat ole' gater don't tink 'bout other people's needs, him. He jest gits it into his head dat he has ta do something and everything else is forgotten." I looked at her sheepishly and said, "So you know about our trip?" She smiled, "Chere, I know 'bout everything dat goes on her; dis is my island."

Not knowing what else to say to her, I explained what we were going to do. "We thought it might be fun to make the trip to California to get my things by the sea because it is something I have never been able to do before. It should only take a couple of weeks and we will be back soon." She just nodded and looked out at the water.

Taking advantage of not having to keep the secret anymore, I asked her, "Can you explain this to Jamie for me? Somehow she misunderstood that this was a guy thing and had nothing to do with how I feel about her and she's sort of mad at me." Stella laughed, "She always was a hothead, her, wearing her heart on her sleeve. She is loud and mean sometimes 'cause she is trying ta

95

hide her vulnerable side. Ah'll talk to her for ya, Chere. You go on an don't keep that overgrown lizard waitin."

Feeling much better about the whole thing, I took off for the beach. When I got there, Jean was pulling the Witch's Bane into the water with chains. I guess he had gathered the ends into his mouth and rolled them around his body. I threw the bags onto the ship, hoping that I didn't break anything, stripped off my shoes and helped him pull. The tide was coming in, but we still weren't getting anywhere. Grunting and huffing, we were both killing ourselves with the effort.

Suddenly the ship began to slide forward into the sea like a hot knife through butter. We had to run to get out of the way. Both of us stunned and trying to figure out what happened, when Max came lumbering around the other side. "Hey dudes, why didn't you tell me you needed a push? You woke me up with all the racket you were making."

Standing there with my mouth hanging open, I had completely forgotten about the dragons. Jean had untangled himself from the chains and realized he had made the same mistake.

"Where you guys goin', anyway?" I laughed and told him that I was going to go on my first sailboat ride to California to get my stuff. I looked at Jean and he popped his head up at me in understanding and I asked the young dragon if he wanted to come along on our cruise. He thought about it for a minute and said, "Naw, you guys go ahead and have fun. I'm workin on something here right now." Jean snorted and thought loud enough for us both to hear, "You mean you are trying to woo that little fish girl, Splash. You have your work cut out for you, Mon Amie. There have been several of her own kind that has tried to catch her attention, but she has rejected all of them so far. She has even eaten a few." Max grinned and sighed in his toothy dragon kind of way, "Yeah, ain't she beautiful?" Jean looked back at me and said, "Mon dieu, he's got it bad. At least she can't eat him."

Jean looked back and started cursing, "Sacre bleu! We've been standing her jawjacking and let our ship drift away from us! Hurry, swim for it!" Max cleared his goo-goo eyes for a minute and said, "Hey, I got this! You guys need a lift?" We both turned to him and I said, "Cool!"

He jumped in the air, swooped around in a circle and grabbed me under the arms in one of his claws and dropped me onto the deck. He circled back around and found Jean in the water swimming toward the boat and used both claws and lifted him out of the water as well.

"Dude! What have you been eating? You're a lot heavier than you look!" Max grunted and eased Jean down onto the deck as well. Jean grunted back at him, "Muscle, Mon Amie, its all muscle." Max laughed and was airborne again. He called to us and said, "If you guys get into any trouble, just shout and I'll have your backs."

I waved him off and turned back to Jean, "Ok, what do I do first?" Jean started barking orders at me in a language I couldn't understand. I told him to stop and said, "Ok, the front of ship is called the bow and the back is called the stern, right?" Jean hissed and thrashed his tail around for a minute and then looked at me and grunted a few times. We went to each rope, sail, hook and plank on the boat and as I touched it, he gave me the name for it.

About two hours later, we were

underway. It was great, the sky was clear and the smell and spray of the ocean made me feel free and exhilarated. Jean had me running all over the place, climbing the rigging, checking this and that, coiling the ropes to his specifications. He was teaching me how to use the wheel to steer and the stars to navigate. After a while when everything was set, I had a few minutes to rest. The water was gentle and calm. The constant rocking of the boat and the sun and wind on my face soothing. I watched as the last tiny speck of land disappeared from view. I imagined what anyone seeing us would say about the antique we piloted across the water. I was trying to figure out what I would tell them when I noticed that the wind was picking up.

Once again, Jean started barking orders. The sea, no longer calm and gentle. The whitecaps of waves began cresting and blowing spray into my face. The old ship creaking and groaning from too many years in dry-dock. Jean told me to trim the sails and start securing items on the deck that had begun rolling about.

Not long after, the sun suddenly was enveloped by angry black clouds.

Lightning began to flash in the distance and I began to worry a little. Jean never gave me any indication that he was worried, so I just assumed this was just a little storm we would have to ride out.

A few more hours passed and the rain pelted the deck like bullets. The little ship was tossed about like a loose car on a roller-coaster. My head began to swim and I had already lost yesterday's dinner...three times. I kept hearing the theme song from Gilligan's island... "And the tiny ship was lost."

As I moved about and made the changes to the rigging that Jean ordered, he would hold the wheel steady with his massive jaws until I could return. He was repeatedly mumbling and cursing about landlubbers. The ship pitched and bounced and as we came down another wave crashed onto the deck, nearly washing me overboard. I screamed at Jean, "Where are the life jackets!" Jean screamed back at me, "What's a life jacket! We don't have time for fashion; we are in the middle of a hurricane! You have to be quick and do what I say or we will be having our dinner with Davey Jones!" I ran to grab the wheel again so he could scramble around and see what else needed to be done.

Standing there, I began to get dizzy; I had already thrown up several times and felt like I needed to again. Jean wasn't close enough to hold the wheel so I could go to the rail, so I began to dry heave while I stood there... or tried to stand. This went on for what seemed like an eternity when the sea began to calm down again. The clouds started to break up and I could see the stars and realized that night must have fallen. Jean took the wheel and told me to go below and rest but to be ready because we were in the eye now and it would start up again at any time. I didn't wait around for him to change his mind. I dove for the old bunk and passed out.

I vaguely remember Jean screaming and tugging on me at some point. Dehydrated and exhausted, I just couldn't seem to wake up. The Dramamine pills I had purchased, just in case, were spilled all over the cabin floor. I woke with some of them stuck to my face on one side and seawater sloshing all around me.

The ship was still. Finally. Sunlight was pouring into the cabin from the porthole and I got up and stumbled up the steps to the deck. I lurched around still weak, examining the damage. Several sails were shredded and one mast was cracked. Debris was everywhere. I even stepped on a dead tuna that must have been washed up by the waves.

I looked everywhere and couldn't find the old alligator. As I neared the wheel, I saw a man lying slumped over it naked as the day he was born. I screamed, "Who are YOU and where is JEAN!" The man didn't move. I thought that he might be dead and went over to him and reached out with my mind. His thought pattern and rhythm felt oddly familiar. He was alive but unconscious.

I was genuinely worried about my best friend. I began to panic, thinking that he might have been washed overboard, when I remembered that he was amphibious and could definitely hold his own in the water. I paced the deck, lost in my panic, when the naked man began to moan and wake, flopping around on the deck.

I ran over to him and shook him hard, "Where is the alligator and how did you get on this ship!" His eyes opened and finally, barely finding his voice he said, "Oh, now you wake! I tried everything to get your sorry ass up! I nearly let the ship capsize trying to get you out of that damned bed!" He licked his lips and croaked out, "Water, I... need... water."

The voice was Jean's voice. The tone of voice and the mental feel of his irritation felt like Jean in my head. Holy Shit! Jean was human again. In my excitement, I dropped him where I had been holding his head, helping him to drink the water I brought. His head hit with a thunk and he reached up to touch it and saw his hand. His human hand. He screamed.... I screamed. He jumped to his feet and felt his chest and arms. He closed his eyes and checked his groin to find it all intact and screamed some more.

We continued to run around in circles screaming. We hugged each other and he winced and drew back. He looked at me and said, "Two hundred years with a hide that a knife couldn't pierce and I have to get the lily white skin of an aristocrat! Hahaha! I'll take it!"

I laughed and told him that I had some burn cream and sunblock in my things that he could use. He walked to the cabin on wobbly legs and giggled at his toes. When he walked in, he said that he thought he would never see this

room again. He had been too big to
even get through the hatch when he was
a gator - that's why he couldn't wake me
up. All he could do was hiss and grunt
at me, he couldn't get in to shake me or
touch me. I gave him my extra pair of
pants and we pulled up chairs that had
been toppled over by the storm and he
told me to reach into a cabinet that was
high on the wall and get his things.

I reached up and pulled out maps
and charts, a sextant, spyglass, books
and other things that had been stored
there. I grabbed more water for us both
and we sat down to try to determine
where we were. He said that from the
stars and the sun and the direction of
the currents, he reasoned that we had
been blown more than halfway across
the Atlantic toward the African Coast.

Recognizing where he pointed to on
the map, I told him that area was near
Guinea and Liberia. I explained that it
had been ravaged by wars and military
conflicts for many years. I told him that
I had actually done some field reporting
on a conflict in Freetown, Sierra Leone.
I explained that I had seen armies of
young boys with automatic rifles fighting
with insurgents in a war for power. By
my calculations we would be heading

straight for it and there had been reports of pirating on civilian vessels in that area.

He smiled and said, "I've been human only a day and I find out that I get to fight pirates too! I have been truly blessed this day." Jean went on still grinning in anticipation, "Did you bring your swords?" I blinked, a little embarrassed by the fact that I never let them out of my sight and nodded. He laughed and rubbed his palms together and said, "Just like old times. If we want to avoid them, we can stop off here at the Cape Verde islands and pick up enough provisions without having to go all the way to the mainland. Now that I'm human again, there is no reason to hide or avoid anything, yes?"

I explained that this ship was now considered a priceless antique and could be more valuable on the black market than drugs or guns. And speaking of drugs and guns, this ship would be perfect for just such an undertaking as the hold was empty and would not be suspected as such. I also added that it wasn't a registered vessel, so that would make it even more appealing to pirates. Jean just smiled and said, "Yes, she is a beauty, no?" I just shook my head at the gleam in his eyes, knowing it meant trouble.

He asked me to tell him what provisions I had brought on board. I dumped the bag that Stella had given me and the food stuff I had stored on board while we were making repairs. He said that there was not enough for two men to turn back. We had to continue on to Africa for more provisions. We were only four or five days away but we only had enough water for one more day.

Proud of myself for thinking ahead, I grabbed the little survival kit I bought on a whim. I showed him the water purification tablets and explained to him how they worked. I showed him the flashlight and other things it contained. He looked at them with awe and wonder. He explained that through the years he was aware of the technological advances that had been made with motors, cars, airplanes and things, because he could see them from the water. The small things like these were never near or close to the water's edge, so he had no idea.

I used one of the empty water bottles and showed him how the tablets worked. He took a drink and nearly spat it out, cursing that it was worse than swamp scum and still salty, but it would be palatable if we boiled it and collected the condensation until we could get more supplies. Potable, I corrected, explaining the term for water that was used for making water ready for human consumption. I looked around and asked how we were supposed to build a fire on a wooden boat. He shook his head and pointed to a small iron pot on legs and said, surely you have used grills before? He shook his head and we began to put the ship to rights. I noticed that I had finally gotten my sea legs and moved about more easily than I had before.

10 ALLIANCES CAREFULLY FORGED

They drove northwest toward Baton Rouge, took some side roads and arrived in a wooded area overlooking a steep hill. The vampire had driven his car, a Maserati. He bottomed out the speedometer, weaving in and out of traffic with reflexes only a computer program could duplicate.

Brady had no desire to speed his

death along, having just escaped imminent death hours before. He closed his eyes and braced himself for impact. What did the vampire care, he was already dead. If he survived this meeting with Queen Mab, he would volunteer to be a designated driver from now on.

It all looked peaceful enough, a little clearing in the middle of the forest, a hill dotted with flowers here and there and the sun shining, almost focusing a beam of light to highlight the little mound. Who would imagine that this was the entrance to the lair of one of the most terrifying creatures that has ever inhabited this planet?

They approached the mound and Brady whistled a whimsical little tune. A hole appeared in the side of the hill. As they approached, it became clear that it was a tunnel, a very well used tunnel, with strong fortifications and bracing. Brady stepped forward to enter and experienced bone searing electric shock that held him in place. His body began to sizzle and smoke. The vampire sighed and jerked him back outside.

Brady lay on the ground still smoking and twitching. The vampire announced himself, "Mab, Queen of all Faekind; I,

Haulfgaard Snoreeson, have answered your request for an audience. With your permission, I ask for admission to this Faerie Sidhe and for safe passage for my journey to you and request to return to this spot on my departure at my discretion, should it please the queen."

A troll lumbered forward out of the darkness to escort the vampire to his destination. Another troll materialized and picked Brady up and hauled him over his shoulder to follow the vampire and his escort.

Trolls were large creatures that stood at least eight to ten feet tall. They had legs the size of tree trunks, they had the lumbering gate and long hanging arms swinging that resembled very large gorillas. Some were hairy; some were covered in boils or warts. It all depended on where they had been when they were born as they incorporated elements around them for substance. Only older, mature trolls had the capability of independent thought. The younger trolls were used as workhorses, muscle and soldiers.

They were led through a maze of darkened tunnels before they were brought to a large room. A woman was lying, practically nude, on a large pallet of furs and skins. She was being fed fruits by a large, also nearly nude man in chains. There were deep scars and fresh welts all over his body.

She had long snow white hair that was arranged into a jeweled fan, like a crown that rested on the top of her head. It was designed to follow the contours of her face and down her neck and shoulders to wind around her body, almost covering her breasts, then down her stomach, to her legs, all the way to her toes, as if it were part of her body.

She had pointed ears, upturned eyes, reminiscent of humans of Asian descent, and long graceful limbs that suggested that she was Elfish. As she moved, she appeared to be in a kind of drunken stupor and completely unaware of her surroundings. It was then that the vampire realized that this creature was not Mab, but merely a distraction.

He began to look around the room to discover a much older woman sitting in a chair watching him. Upon meeting her eyes, her only response was to slightly raise one eyebrow. She was clothed in a finely jeweled cloak that appeared iridescent with her slightest movement. She too wore a headdress. Though not the elaborate machination of the drunken woman; the craftsmanship was finer, less gaudy and designed to fit the contours of her entire head excluding only her face.

Impossible to discern the woman's age, it was apparent that she was past the blush of youth, but with a classic timeless beauty. It was her eyes that made you realize her power. The term 'poker face' had to have been coined from someone who met this woman and survived the encounter. Absolutely without expression, you experienced a mixture of malevolence, humor, good will and strength.

The vampire made these observations and calculated his response in a matter of seconds. Turning his body in her direction, he acknowledged his host immediately. With a slight nod of her head, she beckoned him to approach.

Upon arriving at her chair he bowed slightly from the waist in a show of respect and not the blubbering bending of the knees and kissing of the feet as those who seek gifts or pardons for sins in a sign of submission. His actions gave respect without relinquishing his own power or purpose.

She again gave a slight nod and acknowledged the intent of his bow and turned her attention to Brady, who had been dumped into a heap at her feet. Brady, on the other hand, had fallen into the pose of the blubbering submissive. Completely prostrate with his forehead touching the floor, he waited for his fate.

Several moments of silence followed when she finally spoke. Her voice quiet and strong, she addressed Brady formally, "Bradan Bauchan, son of Calach, King of Boggarts, explain your actions."

Brady blubbered and spoke so fast it was hard to understand what he was saying, "Queen Mab, I have acted as leader to my clan in an attempt to extract vengeance for the murder of my eldest son and the disrespect for the Fae in the land that the queen herself gave to our kind to thrive and grow our race. I beg your forgiveness for failure to defeat those with more power and resources than I possess. I humbly ask, once again, that the queen favor me with her kindness and generosity with the tools that I need to make those pay for those trespasses against the Fae and reinstate the power and influence required for our queen in these new times of awakening."

It was the vampire's turn to raise an

eyebrow. Brady was smarter than he gave him credit for. You didn't survive as the leader of a Fae clan, even one as lowly as a boggart, without skills and resources. He stored that little insight for future reference and reminded himself not to underestimate the little man when it came to issues of power, nor his desperation and greed.

He turned his attention back to the queen to gauge her reaction to Brady's pleas. Calmly she replied, "Bradan Bauchan, you have committed several crimes against Fairie. Your charges are: unauthorized use of a species in an act of war without sanction from your queen, knowledge of acts against Fairie without immediate and full disclosure to your queen, engaging in war without sanction from your queen, consorting with enemies of Fairie without consent from your queen and several other lesser crimes to be listed upon your punishment. How do you plea?"

Without a moment's hesitation, Brady responded, "Not guilty, my queen." Clearly surprised that he would deny the charges, her eyes widened and began to glow, she leaned forward and said quick and sharp, "Plead your case carefully boggart, you are fortunate to have this opportunity for one last chance to escape a life of eternal torment."

Brady swallowed and rose to his knees and raised his eyes to hers for judgment. "I plead not guilty, my queen, to all the charges. When knowledge of all the injustices came to my attention, on the twenty-eighth day of Elembiuos and the hazel moon, I sent my messenger and a gift, a fertile female for my queen, for she was most fair with the blush of youth upon her, the daughter to my mate's sister. I sent her to the Sidhe with the details of events unfolding. I detailed my plan of action for retaliation and asked that should her highness have objection, to send the child back to me as answer to my request. I beseech my queen test these words for their truths." A cup was immediately placed before his lips and he spat into it and it was presented to Mab.

The woman moved so fast it was almost electrifying. Only the vampire's own heightened reflexes followed her movements and only barely so. She moved from her chair across the room and grabbed some herbs and soil and dropped them into the cup. She looked up only an instant and spat into the cup herself. Nothing happened for a moment, then a very fine wisp of smoke rose from the cup for just an instant.

Brady held his breath and waited. Mab strolled slowly back to her seat swirling the contents of the cup. Seated, she looked once more into the cup and stretched out her arm as if handing it to someone and released the cup into the air and it promptly vanished.

She purred back to Brady, "Your words do have a certain small grain of truth to them. You have saved your skin this time by your shrewdness and foresight, for protection in the event of disaster." She looked away and Brady slowly released the breath he had been holding.

Mab turned quickly back to Brady and he jumped, "HOWEVER, Bauchan, you will have to redeem yourself for sending such an important missile at the very day of the storms of my awakening."

She turned to the vampire to clarify her meaning. "Hurricane Katrina made landfall on August 29, 2005. Any attempt by a child with no magical abilities to traverse the terrain in the wake of my storm was sure to meet with failure. Ever sly, the boggart planned for this in his careful wording to give credence to his crimes without any possible recrimination."

She was silent for a few minutes, "No matter, what is done cannot be undone without greater cost than I care to spend. Haulfgaard Snoreeson, of Royal Viking descent, we have a mutual enemy. I find that an alliance for a time is to my liking. What say you, vampire?"

The vampire stood, silent, never taking his eyes off the woman before him. He answered quietly, choosing his words very carefully, "Mab, Queen of Faerie, I find that we may have mutual goals and agree that a temporary alliance may be reached, provided both parties goals be satisfied without harm to the other. Once those goals are specifically met, the alliance would be terminated under an agreement of good will, with no further debt to the other, free to continue on the path of their choosing without interference from the other."

Mab's eyes glittered and she smiled for the first time, revealing the wickedly sharp teeth designed for tearing flesh. She licked her lips in anticipation, with the forked tongue of a serpent. "Wisely spoken, vampire, so shall it be done. The details of our alliance will be negotiated and agreed on by the dawn of the third day of your return to the human world from this moment."

The vampire responded in an important display of fearlessness, "Also wisely spoken. Let our negotiations proceed accordingly; so it is agreed."

Brady and the vampire returned to the spot where they had parked the car, only to find a large boulder in its place. They were in store for a long walk and Brady began complaining immediately.

11 THE GREEN-EYED MONSTER

Jamie and the girls woke to the sounds of falling trees, and the ground shaking and a woman yelling something. She jumped up and ran outside and followed the sounds of battle to the swamp.

MaMere had taken the form of Tethys and she was pissed! She had made a clearing in a densely forested part of the swamp. Huge trees had been uprooted and she was currently using one as a club, swinging it like a baseball bat, pounding the ground with it and screaming in a foreign language at the top of her lungs.

Timing her movements and dodging trees, Jamie ran up to Tethys to grab hold of her and try to talk her down. Tears streaming down her face, she fell to the ground and began to throw another tantrum. Kicking and screaming, she cried, cursing until she was hiccupping and spent. Jamie sat with her the whole time and stroked her hair and soothed her until she was done.

Jamie reached for her with her mind and asked what was wrong. Tethys rose slowly from the ground and began to dust herself off. They sat cross legged on the ground and after a time and Tethys began talking, still crying softly. "He's gone again and I don't know if he will ever come back to me now." Jamie, not sure who she was talking about, asked, "Who's gone?" Tethys wailed, "Jean! He's gone and he's on that damned boat of his! He loves that thing more than he ever loved me! Once he gets far enough he'll figure it out and I'll never see him again!"

Jamie hugged her close to her and rocked back and forth. "Of course he will come back. Jean loves you. He never stopped loving you, even when you turned him into an alligator." Then Tethys began wailing again, "Ohhh, you don't understaaannndd! When huhuhe gets fafafar enough away from me he wawill be hahahuman again and he will have his freedom AND that damned babababoat!"

Jamie sat back, beginning to understand. "You mean he has always had the power to be human? All he had to do was leave the island?" Tethys nodded, buried her head on Jamie's shoulder and cried some more. After a little while longer, she quit her crying hiccups and continued, "He's the only man I ever loved, even if he was human. I knew that he would never live very long, doing the things he was involved in, so when he lost his temper, it gave me the perfect excuse to change him and halt his aging process and keep him with me always." Then she lapsed into another crying fit.

After more tears and a running nose, Jamie's pajama top was completely saturated. She straightened and became more coherent again. "I never expected him to put aside his pride and make his way in the world in the form of an alligator. He could have been human here too if he would have been able to control his temper."

"I found him lying on the beach several times as a human, asleep and calm. I had to alter a gnome once to make him look like a handsome man flirting with me to make Jean's temper flare so he would change back before he realized he was human again. That poor gnomes' wife still won't look at me. Another time, Lynne saw us from the air with her sharp eyesight and asked me in front of Jean who the naked man was she saw me talking to. His jealousy returned in abundance, mission accomplished."

Jamie began to laugh and shake her head in disbelief, "You're jealous!" Tethys sputtered indignantly, "I don't know what you're talking about." Jamie began to laugh so hard she was rolling on the ground. "You are just as bad as he is! You are just as jealous as he is; he's not the only green-eyed monster around here! Wait; doesn't that make you a hypocrite?" Tethys rounded on Jamie, "I AM NOT JEALOUS!"

Adey stepped forward from the spot

where she and Maddie had been watching and said in that weird grown up voice, "You are jealous and insecure and always have been when it comes to that man. Where do you think Calypso got her temper from?"

Maddie stepped up as well and told her, "A man used to adventure and activity can never be held to one spot unless he is offered his freedom to choose to come back to the ones he loves. You cannot force it."

Tethys stood up and brushed herself off. She folded her arms and paced back and forth a couple of times. Jamie spoke up and said, "You know, the girls are right. You can't keep him here forever and expect him to like it. I mean after all, he IS a pirate."

"Speaking of pirates, Dan left with Jean and was trying to keep it a secret from me all along, wasn't he?" Tethys nodded, "So it had nothing to do with wanting to get rid of me, did it?" Tethys said, "No, he asked me to explain it to you before he left, but you were sleeping and....I sort of got distracted by my own grief." Jamie mumbled to herself, "Uh, oh, looks like I have some 'splainin to do, Lucy."

Tethys sat down on one of the

uprooted trees and said, "When I first met Jean, he hadn't been pirating for very long. Born an aristocrat, he watched his entire family guillotined during the French Revolution, when he was only sixteen. When his family was captured, he and his older brother, Pierre, were hidden by servants until they could get out of the country. They signed on as deckhands with a privateer. Both of them had helped with their fathers' shipping ventures and were practically raised on a ship.   It was only a natural course of events that after a couple more years they took over the ship when the crew mutinied."

"Jean was enthralled by America and all that they were fighting for. He still had to earn a living, though, and he did what he does best. He did try to earn an honest living after the president pardoned him, but he had made too many enemies by that time. I convinced him that he could live here with me and never be bothered again. He was happy for a while, but the sea called to him. It was in his blood. He tried to get me to go with him, but I had responsibilities here."

"His favorite ship was a little schooner. It was fast and light. When he built it, he named it the Sea Nymph in honor of me, but I hated it because it was always taking him away where I couldn't follow. He renamed it after a particularly bad argument (I told him I would never step foot on it) the Witch's Bane."

Maddey asked her, "Why can't you leave?" Tethys said, "It's a clause in my deal with God. I guard certain things until the time comes that he tells me to release them. I can go for short periods of time, but I have to find someone worthy to accept my powers, guard the island and relinquish them on my return. The last time I was able to leave the island, Jean was off pirating and he sent me an angel to babysit the place. That's when I found Hawk and brought him home. When I returned, the payment God required of me was to leave a newly born angel into my care."

Wincing at the reference to her Mother, Jamie asked, "How long can you be gone?" Tethys sighed, "Only for one lunar cycle." Jamie said, "That's roughly one month or 27 days, right?" "Yes" she answered.   Jamie thought about it for only a minute and said, "I'll do it." Tethys laughed and said, "It's not as simple as that. You have to learn how to control that much power or it will destroy your mind. You also have to be able to make judgment calls that will not violate my agreement with the Lord."

"So teach me!" Jamie answered her. Tethys shook her head in dismay. Jamie continued, "I am the daughter of an angel, I know and love God. I love you like the mother I never had. There is nothing here on this island that would ever tempt me. Do you have anyone better in mind?"

Tethys looked at Jamie and started thinking. "You know, it might just work if you could stay out of trouble." Jamie huffed, "I haven't caused any trouble in a very long time and I resent my past always being thrown in my face."

Tethys, Maddie and Adey gave Jamie the 'yeah, right, look.' Jamie defended herself, "Well, not any trouble I actually caused anyway... on purpose."

Tethys touched her chin and said, "If I only took short trips, no more than a day or two... short of blowing up the planet, you couldn't ruin anything too big that I couldn't fix when I got back." Jamie brightened, "That's the spirit!" Tethys started walking back to the house, laughing, and said, "Come on young lady, you have a lot to learn."

Jamie laughed too and said, "You know, there might be a thing or two I could teach you, too." Tethys stopped in her tracks and said, "What do you mean you could teach me?"

Jamie reached up and lifted the hem of her tunic and said, "If you want to catch bees you have to know what honey to use."

12 NO TIME FOR LIZARD BOY

Splash was so mad she was blowing bubbles from her gills. Max was stalking her again. Every time she turned around, he was there. She was going to have to talk to Jamie again and tell her to keep lizard boy out of her way or she was going to…. do something; she just didn't know what yet.

The last time she had had to talk to Jamie, he had been frightening the young ones and ruining their fishing grounds. This time it was just the opposite. He was like a pied piper playing games with the little ones. They followed him around everywhere he went and that usually meant wherever she was.

She was trying to settle a territory dispute at the moment between two matriarchs. Both had eligible daughters for mating to a Potomoi and they were haggling over rights to a particular spawning area of flounder and sea skates. She was having a hard time finding out what was so special about the male that had both families competing for him. She was concentrating on what the real issue was when she was swarmed by a pod of children trying to tickle her with their fins. Somehow they had also obtained the notion that she was ticklish. The children or, wogs, didn't develop legs until after they had reached puberty, in much the same way a tadpole has a tail and grows legs. They swarmed all around her, wriggling their little tails all over her with great delight.

She didn't have time for this; she

was the governor of the Nereids, eldest daughter to the queen. It was her responsibility to see her race flourish and grow. That meant settling disputes, assigning territories, leading her people to better fishing grounds and protecting them from danger.

Several hours later, she had concluded her business with the matriarchs and was on her way to find Jamie. She had to make Lizard Boy go away for good. She had just reached Tethys's beach and called for Jamie. Jamie was already there and she was holding Tethys's staff.

Alarmed, she approached cautiously when Jamie smiled at her and said, "Relax, I'm just filling in for a few days so Tethys can find some alone-time with Jean." Stunned, she was shocked to find out that Tethys had left the island. She hadn't done that since right after she was born and she was far from being a young wog.

Jamie told her that she was in charge for a couple of days. She asked her how that was possible and Jamie told her that she had the right blood to be able to stand the power transfer for a short time to allow the goddess the ability to leave the island for a short period of time without dying.

Confused and shocked Splash almost forgot why she had called for Jamie until she was tripped by a wog playing keep away with the dragon in question and was weaving in and out her legs, using her as a shield. She wobbled and landed face first in the surf coming up with a mouthful of sand and mud.

Her anger refreshed, she came up screeching; her greenish complexion gone completely pink around her face and gills on her chest. She shrieked incoherently that Max had to go or she was going to kill somebody even if she couldn't kill him.

In the middle of her tirade, Max had come to shore, changed and was standing to Jamie's side, grinning like an idiot. This infuriated her even more and she made a lunge for him with her sharp claws. She actually managed to get in a good swipe and scraped him across his face. He blinked and brought his hand up to the scratch to find that he was bleeding. Green blood. Max just stared at it. He had never been wounded before...by anything.

Splash's eyes blazed and she shouted, "I knew it, you ARE vulnerable! Keep hounding me and I will feed you your own scales, Lizard Boy!"

Bubbles, her sister and closest companion for most of her life, came up to stand beside Max. Splash realized that her best friend was now defending him against her. What did she expect, Bubbles was in charge of the wogs and the preservation of their species. She was siding with him! She was so mad she sprayed everyone with seawater and turned and dove into the water and sped away in anger.

Jamie looked at Bubbles and asked her to follow her friend and look after her. Jamie took Max by the arm and led him back to the house to have a look at the scratch that seemed to be bleeding more than it should.

When they got to the house, they met Hawk standing at the door. She started to explain and then realized that he must have heard and seen the whole encounter. Hawk was intrigued at the wound. Max still wasn't speaking. Jamie brought him to the big table to sit down while Hawk dressed his wound. She didn't say a word when she noticed him scooping a couple of drops of dragon blood into a vial and stuffing it in his pocket.

After Max was taped and bandaged

Jamie asked Max why he was bothering Splash so much. Max just looked at the ground and shrugged his shoulders still not saying anything. Exasperated, Jamie said, "We've gone over this Max, you have to quit bugging her and yet you keep right on doing it. Why?" Max just looked at Jamie like any teenage boy would when they are called into the principal's office. Jamie stared back at him waiting for some kind of explanation.

Hawk cleared his throat and patted Max on the shoulder, "I think I can help the situation by giving this guy a little change in scenery. Jace and Justin have been moping around since the Hell storm and Lynne pulled everyone close to home till things have calmed down a little while. How 'bout it big guy, you want to go hang out with a bunch of rowdy guys looking to burn off some steam?"

Max smiled, stood up and said, "Lead the way, chief." Jamie looked at Hawk and told him to make sure to have the boys keep him out of trouble; she had enough to deal with right now without having to worry about damage control for her dragon.

Hawk turned to Jamie, threw his

head back and howled laughing. He was nearly doubled over when Jamie told him that she didn't know what he was laughing at and she didn't think the situation was funny at all.

Her statement only made him laugh harder. When he finally got himself under control, he said that MaMere had always told him that what comes around goes around and that everything in life is circular. She had told him that when he had gone to her complaining about Jamie and his frustration with trying to keep her out of all the troubles she got into in her youth.

He said that she had told him that many times, but never thought he would see the day when it actually happened. He would remember this moment for the rest of his life. Jamie kicked him in the shin and stomped down the hall.

Hawk met Max in the yard and they both jumped into the air, completing their changes in flight. Max communicated telepathically to Hawk that he noticed he wasn't ripping clothing off before he changed anymore. Hawk replied that when they were in battle during the Hell storm, Sam would transform with her clothing intact and explained that once she had the original items of clothing, she just imagined putting them in a pouch under her skin so that she could access them with her mind when she needed to change back. The transfer back and forth was a displacement of mass and that the ability to become animals with different body mass required pulling from the molecules around them to store and pull from when needed.

He began to think about what she said, so he tried imagining putting his clothes under his feathers as well. It didn't really work right the first couple of times he tried it, but with practice he finally got it right.

Max chuckled and said all you guys think about things way too much. If you see the world with infinite possibilities, then all things are possible. You got to be positive, dude. Hawk laughed and told him that he might have a point and they flew to Hawk's place.

What a difference a day makes. Jace and Justin had introduced Max to the world of dirt bikes. With their enhanced abilities, they had the balance and strength that humans could never achieve. Constantly sneaking off to compete with humans or use the motocross tracks, they had become veritable legends in the motocross world. This is not a good thing for supernatural creatures with a big secret.

Showing up at the last minutes before a race they had also achieved a certain amount of notoriety of being mysterious and unpredictable. Lynne had forbidden them to compete because of the attention they received and their unfair advantage. When they won, which they usually did, prizes were always donated to under-privileged youth programs.

Max was also a natural, with abilities equal to or greater than their own. Max was accustomed to great speeds, heights and enormous depths, but he had never experienced these things on a machine and certainly never in human form.

Justin and Jace had finally found a competitor worth competing against. The three of them had scoured far and wide, looking for abandoned tracks or natural terrain that would provide a worthy challenge when they found it. Find it they did; a series of natural mounds surrounding a much larger one. The slopes were perfect for jumping. As soon as the three of them spotted the mounds in the distance, they didn't bat an eye and raced forward, eager for the experience.

13 WHAT NOT TO WEAR

Jamie and Tethys walked arm in arm back to the house, laughing and talking about the men they cared about. When they got back, Tethys took a great deal of time showing Jamie how to use power and direct it with the staff. She tried to explain to Jamie just how dangerous having that much power could be. Jamie could kill or cause great destruction with just a thought, so she had to concentrate to control her emotions.

After several practice attempts, Jamie was able to replant the uprooted trees Tethys had vented with and repaired all the damage to the surrounding area. Tethys told her, "If nothing else, you can fix broken things. That's mostly what I use the staff for on a regular basis." She couldn't materialize objects without merging them together. A boat paddle was stuck in a boulder much like the sword in the stone. Tethys told her that she shouldn't need to materialize anything unless they were attacked or in trouble. She shouldn't be gone long enough for that to happen.

Tethys told her to try not to use any power at all unless she had absolutely no other choice. With any luck, nothing would happen and Jamie would have just wound up house-sitting for her. Yeah....right. Who was she kidding; she just hoped she wouldn't kill anyone before her return.

Before she relinquished her powers, she called for Asia and Phoros. Their names, in honor of the old gods of death Euthanasia and Thanatophoros, were killer whales that had served Tethys for many years, and would take her to where Jean and Dan were.

When they arrived, she started to go to them and waded out in the water stumbling considerably due to the lack of enormous physical strength she was normally accustomed. The simple act of walking became an exercise in itself. She stepped on something sharp in the water and she experienced pain, real stinging pain. She had seen the effects on others, of course, but she had never even had so much as a paper cut. This might be a little more difficult than she thought.

She tried to mount the animals the way she had seen Jamie do and found that she lacked the upper body strength to hold herself up until they gained enough momentum to allow her to stand. (Much like someone fanning-out when standing up on water skis.) After several failed attempts, she finally gave up and straddled the great mammal and held on to her fin to ride along in the water. She hoped Dan and Jean hadn't gone very far, she didn't know how long she could hang on like this. Fortunately her new make-over wetsuit/femme fatal armor that Jamie had designed for her kept her from seriously chafing.

She fidgeted with the material, nervous as to what Jean's reaction might be to her new look. Missing her staff, she thought about all the preparations she had made before she relinquished her powers. Jamie told her that the white toga clad, gauntleted warrior woman look went out with Xena and was just considered tacky now. Jamie told her that the she was going to make her look like a, "bad ass bitch" that would strike fear in her enemy's eyes and desire in a man's groin.

Tethys wasn't sure she wanted to be referred to as a bitch, but apparently the term was accepted now as a testament to a woman's fortitude and strength of character by many in today's culture. She tried to explain to Jamie that she was trying to impress Jean Lafitte, one of the greatest pirates of the 18th century, whose last experience with feminine fashion was ruffles and lace-in abundance.

Jamie's reply to that was, "Look, he didn't choose lace and ruffles and those other weak females, he chose you. You do want to make him sit up and take notice, don't you? Make him remember what he is leaving all alone on this little island. This outfit will make him do more than just sit up in his chair, if you catch my drift."

She was skeptical, but she relented and let Jamie make her changes. At first it felt odd and a little uncomfortable with all the straps and things that clung to her body like a glove. However the boots made her legs feel strong and supported. Jamie insisted that the design incorporate at least a three inch heel. Tethys argued that it wouldn't be practical and would hamper her movements considerably.

Once the overall look was accomplished, Jamie stepped back and told Tethys to look at herself in the mirror. Jamie had taken her mane of dark hair and braided it in small braids that clung close to her scalp and piled high on her head in a ponytail to cascade down her back to her rear end. She had woven leather, colored yarns and other objects into the braids as well. Upon further inspection, Tethys discovered that some of the items were small weapons for "just in case," as Jamie put it, and were disguised as adornments.

The clothing left little to the imagination. Boots were designed to fit her legs like a second skin with soft soles that were actually comfortable on her feet. Made out of a breathable durable fabric similar to neoprene, but constructed out of spider silk and dyed sharkskin for an indestructible, waterproof and stretchy material. There was a little catch on the instep of each sole that would release fins for swimming. A compromise was reached regarding the heels. They were designed so that they would flip up over the back to allow her to be able to walk, run or swim easily. However, Tethys had to concede to having them rise above her knees.

The boots also incorporated clips and pockets that concealed weapons of all kinds, small daggers, throwing stars, wire and other things. Jamie giggled, mumbling something about Batgirl drooling over them. When Tethys looked inside Jamie's mind for the details of all the designs, she reproduced them exactly as Jamie pictured onto herself. The only problem she had was with the actual clothing. Jamie pictured the garments separately and when she produced them as pictured she had difficulty figuring out how to put them on and their purpose.

Jamie explained that the top was designed with a built in corset that would lift and separate but still be flexible. Jamie was pleased to discover that no padding was necessary to reveal just the right amount of cleavage that would be distracting to any male. A short, long-sleeved bolero style jacket was made to match, also made of a lightweight, stretchy fabric. Jamie took out one of her own one piece swimsuits to show her how the bottoms were meant to be worn. Like the swimsuit, it hugged her body and covered her privates, but left only a thin piece of material that went between her buttocks.

Tethys staunchly refused to bare her bottom and they went through several design changes until they finally agreed that the thong would define the shape but would be incorporated into boy-shorts for modesty. Tethys added one more item that at first Jamie argued against, but when presented she was pleasantly surprised and relented.

Tethys came up with a black iridescent skirt that was detachable. Trimmed in pure gold and platinum filigree at the waist, it followed her waistline from the back to a deep 'v' and open in the front. Tethys explained that it would morph into a cloak or shorter skirt, trousers, fins or even gliding wings if the need arose. Jamie smiled, "Cool and very high tech. I would have never thought of that, sort of a mix of old and new with just enough leg showing to make a man sweat.

Tethys was the one sweating right now. She worried if her island would still be intact when she returned. She worried if she would frighten her lover away when he saw her...If, of course, he could even stand to lay eyes on her, now that he had his freedom.

With her telepathy, the only remaining power she didn't have to relinquish, because Jamie already possessed the ability naturally, she constantly searched for Jean. She detected fear and happiness, exhaustion and exhilaration. He had definitely been released from her spell.

She remembered what it was like when they first met. She had watched him smuggling goods in through Barataria Bay. In just a very short span of time, the man had charmed all the women in the area. He kept his crew on the straight and narrow, forbidding any sort of rape or robbery of the locals. In fact, in more cases than not, he actually brought food and supplies to the families of the Cajuns that were in desperate need of supplies due to taxes and embargoes that the governor had imposed. They adored him.

Back then, she had cloaked her little island in a mist that kept others from discovering her tiny treasure island. So during a particularly bad storm, Jean and his crew were surprised and relieved to have been beached on her island before the tiny skiff they were in was overcome in the turbulent waters. She was hesitant to let them beach the little boat, but she was intrigued with his daring and compassion for others. She will never forget the smile on his face when he noticed her watching him from her front porch.

He strolled up, swaggering and smiling, so sure of himself. Then he fell into a gnome trap and it was her turn to smile. She sent a message to the gnomes not to eat him. After two days, she had the gnomes bring him to her. Even after all that, he still had the audacity to try to charm her. Oh, such good times, the fond memory made her sad all over again at the possibility that she had lost him forever now.

To take her mind off her depression, she scanned for Jamie. She found that Jamie was practicing with the power; only one or two small fires had been extinguished so far. The gnomes were working furiously to repair the damage of Jamie's experiments.

Tethys sent Jamie a reminder that the power was not limitless and she would have to remember to recharge frequently if she was going to keep practicing. As an after-thought, she warned Jamie that under no circumstances was she to even approach her books or her kitchen with the power she now possessed. If she accidentally invoked any of the spells that some of those books contained there was no telling what would happen.

At that point she received a feeling of warmth and comfort from Maddie and Adey. Though young girls, they still possessed the balance of power and magic on this planet. They would keep careful watch on their mother and douse all power should she inadvertently wander into danger.

More at ease, Tethys settled into the movements of the whale and the motion of the sea. She had forgotten how much she had missed it all. She had agreed to her guardianship on the island after eons of freedom, thinking that she had done it all and there was nothing new to discover and she was ready to settle down.

During her time on the island in Old Lady Lake, she had spent so much time taking care of others, guiding and nurturing, protecting, as was her nature and the nature of motherhood, or more accurately, grandmother. She had adopted the persona of MaMere for so long that she forgot that she was also a woman...a woman with needs, a woman who reveled in adventure and battle, a woman in love.

14 I'LL SIP ON YOUR BONES FOR MY SUPPER

Justin and Max were in a pickle. Tricked by two Fae, who were disguised as young girls lost in the woods and trapped down the proverbial rabbit hole, they called to the young men to come rescue them. Being the heroes, they jumped at the chance, feet first...right into a magical trap set by Mab herself.

Justin heard their cries for help first and killed the engine so he could hear them better. Jace had gone to see if he could scare up some wild game for lunch and left Max and Justin to continue competing to see who could perform their new stunts the best.

Justin called Max over and told him what he was hearing. Max, being a dragon and not overly fond of humans, was indifferent to the whole thing if he couldn't eat them for his lunch. Justin, however, had been raised with high moral standards and taught to never ignore a cry for help. He whacked Max on the head and said, "Dude, they could be beautiful," and waggled his eyebrows at Max.

Max, grumbled, "Or they could be ugly as cave slugs in rut." Justin looked at him and said, "What's a cave slug? Never mind, I don't want to know. Besides, if Jace gets back and hears their call, and finds out we didn't do anything he will tell my dad." Max, eyes flickering to dragon and back again said, "So." Justin rolled his eyes at him and continued, "My dad, Hawk, will tell my mother and she will whip the snot out of me and then she will tell Jamie."

That was all Max had to hear and he

shifted his arms to claws and began digging. Before they both jumped down into the hole the girls had fallen in, Justin looked at him and said, "Get rid of those things, we don't know if they are human or not. They must be pretty far down 'cause I can't smell anything from here."

Max shifted his arms back to human and told him that Justin owed him a big dinner, and they both took the plunge. Max first and Justin second. As soon as Max's feet touched the ground, he was enveloped in chains. Max roared and was jerked out of the way just in time for Justin to land in his place. Justin was also wrapped in some kind of rope or cable. Justin had begun to change as soon as he heard Max's roar, so he was only partially changed when he landed and was captured. Now he was stuck that way, weak and unable to use his strength, teeth or claws to free them.

They both thrashed and rolled about, but were unable to break themselves free. Max tried to change back to dragon and found that he couldn't. He was stuck. What's more is that he found that the strange chains that had been thrown around him were burning him.

Justin was in a similar predicament,

only his restraints were different. They were ropes wound with herbs. If Max's nose was correct, it was wolfsbane. Justin was just as stuck as he was.

They heard a female begin laughing. Evil and menacing, she cackled, "I knew it! A spirited one and a dragon! This is our lucky day!" The voice was old, but the body it came out of didn't appear to be old or young, just mean.

Max yelled, "I am a direct descendant of Throlldrrr, the mightiest dragon of Atlantis! I am immune to magic! What manner of chains are these that scream in my head and burn this human skin!"

Mab's eyes widened at his words, "You are young in this regeneration cycle, my young dragon friend. Do you not recognize the enemy of your forefathers, Mab, Queen of Fairie? You are being held by the very bones of your ancestors. When I destroyed Atlantis, I retrieved the old bones from the bottom of the ocean and had them carved very carefully to form a chain that I have now used to imprison you with. Everyone knows that the only thing that can kill a dragon is another dragon!"

"We made a deal, your king and I. His world was sinking and all his offspring were dying. He came to me begging for help. I agreed to give him the magic he needed to save them both. The task drained me and all my Fae to the point of being powerless. When I came to claim my prize, he reneged and cursed me to live underground at the mercy of nature and whatever magic seeped through the earth to sustain my race."

"You have literally fallen into my lap. This Sidhe is birthplace of my rise to the topside of the Earth, where I will take over and rule all magic. No longer will I sleep under the Earth existing on the magic of fairy tales for sustenance, for humans have entered a new age of belief. The more they believe, the more magic is produced in the world and I intend to be able to consume it freely once again!"

Max roared and thrashed, welts and blisters beginning to show where the chains touched his skin. Jace yelled, "What manner of prize did you mean to collect, old witch!"

Mab became completely quiet. She glided over to where Jace lay on the ground and bent over slightly at the waist and sniffed deeply. "Not a wolf child, but a spirit child of a canine and avian, a duel spirit. That is very rare. Both your spirit totems are very old, older than any other I have encountered before. Who are your parents, spirited one?

Justin huffed spitefully with great pride and told her, "I am the son of Robert Brown-Wing Eschte, the Great Thunder Hawk, Anasazi of the Hopi and Navajo People. I am the son of Lynne Bordelon, ancestor of Two Shadows, a shaman of the Choctaw Nation and I'm afraid that you have bitten off more than you can chew, lady!" Mab brought her hand out to sprinkle some glittering flakes over him. Wherever they touched his skin, they stuck and smoked his skin. He screamed and twisted in agony.

She continued her story as if Justin's comments were of no consequence. "I was to have eternal beauty and be his queen to rule beside him for all eternity. I loved him and he betrayed me for his precious dragons. It is their bones that would give me eternal life. Now I am reduced to sucking on relics."

"A true gift to one who deserves so much, a fresh, live dragon has been delivered to me. What a wonderful day this is indeed."

Justin barely heard her last words

and giving up the futile fight for consciousness.

15 A GUANTLET IS THROWN

Jace came back from his hunt with a cache of game for the greedy dragon and a couple of rabbits, a hedgehog for Justin and himself. When he got back to the dirt-bike course, he found the bikes, but Justin and Max were nowhere to be found.

Jace changed back to his hawk form and scanned the area. From above he couldn't find them anywhere. He began circling the area where their bikes were and found a small area that had been disturbed. He flew back down for a closer look and found that the grass and dirt were definitely disturbed by human feet. Listening and searching with superhuman sight and hearing, he began to hear yelling from underneath the ground. He changed back to human form and began digging furiously, stopping every so often to listen.

He heard Mab's screeching diatribe and instantly realized that at this point there was nothing he could do to save his brother and his friend. He shifted in a flash and was airborne. He circled the site once to make a mental imprint of the exact location in his brain and made a beeline for his father.
Breathless, he found Hawk near MaMere's island. As soon as Hawk saw his son, he immediately knew something was wrong. Hawk tipped his wing and they both dove for land, changing on the way.

Jamie had just run out onto the front porch and into the yard with her pants on fire. She was dancing around in circles trying to put out the remaining embers still smoking on her boots.

When Hawk and Justin landed with loud thumps it startled her and she jumped and pointed the staff, shooting a bolt of electricity into the air, narrowly missing Hawk's left ear and burning a lock off of his long black hair.

Jace and Hawk didn't even notice she was there. Jamie realized that when Hawk didn't start screaming at her immediately, something was bad wrong. Jace ran to his father and began yelling that some woman had captured Justin and Max and was going to eat their bones. Hawk put his hands on his shoulders to hold him still for a minute and peered inside Jace's mind. The shaman training that he had practiced for centuries proved to be invaluable at this moment. He could clearly search Justin's mind to read his memories and find out just exactly what had happened. The events played out like a movie, every detail completely clear.

As soon as he heard Mab's voice in his son's mind, he paled. He listened to her tell her tale of revenge and domination. Hawk turned to Jamie and yelled, "Where's Stella!"

Jamie had been scanning Jace's mind as well and when she heard Mab's voice, it struck a strange chord in her mind.

Jamie was, after all, part Fae. Mab was the Queen of all Faekind and Jamie reacted like any Fae, with a hypnotic-like trance. Stunned, Jamie had been dazed and didn't even hear Hawk yelling at her to find MaMere. Hawk walked over and grabbed her by the shoulders and was shaking her hard when her head finally cleared.

She blinked and told Hawk that MaMere, Stella, Tethys was gone. She left the island to go find Jean Lafitte. Hawk then looked and saw that Jamie was holding Stella's staff. His eyes already hard with rage, he pointed at the staff and yelled, "What the hell are you doing with that?" At that point Jamie stepped back from him, raised her chin and told him, "I told you, Tethys has left the island to find Jean and she left me in charge until she comes back."

Hawk turned his head and spat on the ground and muttered, "Unbelievable... one of the most powerful wielders of magic in the world has awakened and plans to bring her domain to the topside and she decides to take a vacation. To top it off she leaves you in charge... un-freaking-believable."

He turned to Jace and told him, "Go tell your mother and gather everyone and meet back here. I'm going to try to find someone who might be able to help, but it might take a while." He turned to look at Jamie sternly and said, "I don't care if you're in charge, DO NOT even approach the Sidhe until I return with reinforcements. Do you understand me, girl?"

Jamie huffed and sniped "I'm not a girl, and I am in charge whether you like it or not. Fortunately, I agree with you. I will wait here until you return or Tethys comes back, whichever comes first." Hawk stared threateningly at her for a moment and jumped into the air, Jace, following his father's lead, did the same and they flew off on the horizon.

Jamie turned and was about to go back into the house when she heard a boat motor come roaring into the little cove in front of the house. Aundrea nearly ran over the little dock there in her haste.

She jumped out of the boat and started yelling, "Go get MaMere! Something is wrong with Sam, I think she's dying! There's blood everywhere! ….At least I think its blood." Jamie and Aundrea ran to the boat to find Sam lying naked and drenched in green stuff.

Jamie reached inside Sam's mind

and found the cause of the problem. It was horrific to Sam, pain beyond belief, her heart was fluttering and she was mad at everything. All she wanted to do was cry and eat chocolate.

Jamie searched deeper to find out what was causing the pain. She looked into her cells and organs to confirm her suspicions. As a doctor of molecular biology, she was quite familiar with the biologies of many different species. Dragons were different, but the basics were the same as other reptiles. What she couldn't figure out was why she was also adopting systems of human biological cycles.

Jamie sat back on her haunches and tried to calm Sam and talk to her, "Sam, when did you first start having these pains?" Sam whaled, "Oooohhh about a couple of days agoooo!" Jamie continued to soothe her and asked, "Sam, can you search your memory and tell me how your race determines that you are ready to breed?"

Sam sat straight up, eyes wide open, "Oh HEELLLL NO! It can't be my time! I don't have a viable mate! Dragons find their mates in battle. Only when a male bests the female is he allowed to mate. Most males do not survive the attempt.

The female cannot breed without having consumed the blood of a battle kill. The female is aroused only by an intense fire within that is stoked by fire in the heart. Once her eggs are fertilized, she retreats to lay her eggs, one every ten years, in her lair for the rest of her life. I haven't had a proper battle and even if I did, I haven't smelled the heat of another that is worthy to be my mate.

Jamie said softly, "What about Max?" Sam looked at her like she was dripping in vampire slime and said, "Have you lost your mind? He is my brother! He cannot mate with me because he has our mother's fire in his blood. You humans are sick! Do you know that? If you don't believe me, just ask him!"

Jamie's face paled when Sam asked for her brother. Sam, although out of sorts, didn't miss Jamie's reaction. Sam looked at Jamie through narrowed eyes, "Where is he? I can't feel him in my mind. I know something is wrong, I could feel it the minute these damned stomach pains started coming and then blood gushed from between my legs."

Jamie looked Sam in the eyes and said, "I want you to remain calm. I have something to tell you and I need you not to blast me with your fire breath, ok?" Sam nodded slowly, never taking her eyes of Jamie. Jamie took a deep breath and said, "Max and Justin have been captured by Mab. Hawk has gone to get help and we are going to get him back."

Sam jumped out of the boat and started running around in circles. She was trying to transform and couldn't. She was in a lot of pain, that much was obvious. She would strain and her muscles would tense and she would get a claw or scales and it would bounce back to human form.

Sam began to really panic now. Jamie ran to her and tried to hold her and Sam just pushed her away. Jamie reached for Tethys's staff and pounded it on the ground and the ground rumbled under their feet, knocking Sam flat on her back. Sam, now wild eyed and almost incoherent, got up on her knees and grunted and strained with all her might and her tail appeared, but nothing else. The tail stayed.

Sam was physically and emotionally spent and she collapsed back on the ground whimpering and crying that Max was going to die because she was a damned female with a screwed up reproduction system. She moaned that he had been right all along, teasing her that the only thing that would kill her was being a girl.

Aundrea gathered Sam into her arms and carried her friend to the house, and cleaned her up and put her in one of the spare beds. When Aundrea had Sam resting, she came back out and joined Jamie on the front porch. Funny, she thought to herself, when you talked about love and guidance, you referred to her as MaMere. When you talked about power and battles, they were now beginning to refer to her as Tethys. It just seemed natural for everyone to think that way now that she had revealed herself.

Aundrea said, "Ok, begin telling me what happened from the top so I can figure out what the hell is going on and what is happening to Sam."
Jamie sighed, "From what I can tell about from Sam's explanation of dragon breeding processes, she is in heat. However, she is experiencing symptoms similar to human menstruation cycles. The only thing that makes sense is that when we went into battle during the Hell storm, she must have ingested enough battle blood to start her gestation cycle and when she transformed to human,

those cycles took the only normal route possible, she has started her period."

Aundrea laughed and said, "That does make sense in a way. We were at the beauty shop and she had just had her nails done and she came to me and announced in front of everybody, "Look, Aundy! I had my claws sharpened, don't they look great?"

"I thought I was gonna die of embarrassment. There were a couple of older ladies in the shop that started laughing so hard I thought we were going to have to get them an oxygen machine. As she was showing me her nails, she suddenly started crying about the death of her scales and then she started doubling over in pain. We had to leave the shop. I took her to Aunt Lynne's and made her lie down. She got up later that night and ate every shred of food in the house and when Aunt Lynne got up the next morning and went to cook breakfast and found the mess Sam left, she threw us both out. That was three days ago. We have been camping out in a motel ever since."

Jamie nodded and continued, "Dan and Jean have fixed up Jean's old schooner and have gone on a road trip of sorts and are sailing to California.

When Jean gets out of range of MaMere's power on the island, the spell she cast on him will fall apart and he will be human again." Aundrea turned to Jamie and said, "You mean all this time all he had to do was leave?" Jamie smirked, "Yep, or control his temper around her." Aundrea blew out a deep breath and said, "Yeah, he's got a real temper too. When he figures it out, he's gonna blow his lid. We probably won't ever see him again."

Jamie shook her head and said, "I wouldn't be too sure about that. Tethys's went after him and left her power here with me." Aundrea scooted a little further away from Jamie on the porch where they were sitting and said, "She can really do that? Wouldn't having that much power be dangerous if you didn't know what you were doing?"

Jamie put her head in her hand and said, "Yeees, I have already blown a hole in the roof of the house, sunk MaMere's pirogue, burned two pairs of pants and ruined my best pair of boots... Oh, and I nearly blew Hawk's head off."

Aundrea looked down at her pants and boots, noticing for the first time the condition they were in. Aundrea was a Were and Weres mostly destroy their clothing when they change too much to give fashion much thought, if any. She just said, "I thought you smelled a little charred earlier."

Aundrea was quiet for a moment and continued more seriously, "So Tethy's is incommunicado, Max and my cousin have been captured by Mab. Who's that anyway? Do we have reason to be worried?" Jamie looked out at the water and said, "We have plenty to worry about. Mab is Queen of all Fae and is extremely powerful. She has awakened from her exile and it seems she has decided she needs to get her tan on."

Aundrea shrugged and said, "Well, why is that such a bad idea? I know plenty of Fae folk and they seem pretty decent people from what I've experienced." Jamie replied, "You don't understand. Mab didn't get that much power by sprinkling pixie dust on people. She consumed them and ate their power. You have to remember that Fae means ALL FAE. Trolls, ogres, boggarts, nymphs, sirens, as well as pixies and fairies. There are Fae clans that some have never seen in this millennium and most of them are too scary to even set eyes on. She controls all of them and she is not noted for her generosity and humanitarian efforts."

"Anyway, she has somehow captured Max and Justin in her Sidhe and from what I gather, she wants to have them as an appetizer before she comes topside."

Aundrea was now the one with the worried look. "Has Aunt Lynne been told yet?" Jamie nodded, "Hawk sent Jace to her before he left for reinforcements." Aundrea looked at Jamie and said, "You have the telepathy thingy, why don't you send out an S.O.S.? With the extra power boost from Tethys's power, surely you can reach farther out now."

Jamie thought about it for a minute and said, "You might be right. At this point, what could it hurt? Since I have had so many, uh…miscalculations, why don't you go in the house and keep an eye on Sam and I will go to the other side of the island with this thing, (motioning to the staff) to be on the safe side."

Jamie reached the other side of the island, staff in hand, and began to relax her mind, breathing deeply, taking in all that was around her. She tried to think of the distress call that would bring Tethys back and connect with the killer whales that were her transport. She closed her eyes, raised the staff and sent out what she imagined were thought waves of distress and a call for help. Being near water, she imagined the calling process as a pebble dropped into a bucket of water and the thoughts spreading out like the ripples of water that spread where the pebble was dropped.

She left the call to ripple on the water and stopped the source of energy. She didn't want to overdo it or anything. She waited for a little while and nothing happened. Oh well, it was worth a try and she trekked back to MaMere's house to check on Sam.

16 LIKE WATER RIPPLING OUTWARD

Sam called to her brother through their blood bond. She could feel him and his panic and frustration, but that was it. At least he was still alive. She lay on her side panting from the repeated attempts to change back to her dragon form. The more she tried, the harder the muscle cramps seized her body. She felt the uncontrollable need to cry...tears...human tears. Such weakness of spirit made her feel so ashamed of herself, she was nauseous as well. How could she have let herself get into this position? She lay on the bed, exhausted from her efforts and pain and eventually fell into a fitful, fever induced sleep.

Max struggled and thrashed, pulling on the chains that bound him. Nothing worked. The harder he pulled, the weaker he got. He felt his great inner strength being drained from him. For the first time in his life he was a prisoner, trapped by magic. This wasn't supposed to be possible. Dragons were immune to magic. He was so mad there really was smoke coming out of his nose. He thought being human for a little while was fun when this all started. Being human sucked. He thought about the freedom and power he had always enjoyed in his dragon. There was nothing as bad-assed as he was on the planet, so nothing ever bothered him and he had nothing to fear. His strength was boundless; the entire world was his for the taking. Now look at the mess he was in.

He looked around and saw that he and Justin weren't the only prisoners here. Several other beings were also bound and chained in some manner or another. This part of the Sidhe must be the equivalent of dungeons. As he completed his survey and determined that more than half of the other prisoners were actually dead, he noticed something or someone being held under the rays of a powerful light. Brown and withered, it twitched ever so often toward the shadows, until it had gotten a finger into the darkness beyond the beams of light and his arm began to slowly grow.

A goblin came thumping around the corner and reached out and turned the being so that the parts that had been hidden from the light were now exposed. The goblin noticed the appendage and quickly flipped the new growth into the light once again and mumbled, something about cursed nightshades always slinking about.

The goblin finished with the task of securing the prisoners, lumbered back down the corridor from which he came. Max, trying to conserve his energy only moved his eyes as he continued his survey of his surroundings and noticed the another man chained on the wall watching him as well. A large man, heavily built, obviously strong and from the look in his eyes, he would never be broken. Signs of torture covered his body. He met the man's eyes and saw the spirit within and understood the heart of a warrior.

Suddenly he felt the call of his sister. He concentrated and tried to return her call. He felt like he was in a bubble that dampened the connection. He felt her pain and emotional turmoil. He felt within her mind and found that she had finally been matured by battle and was ready for mating. Max squeezed his eyes shut and tried to send her comfort.

He dreaded this time for a long while. He had hoped that by now they would have found another dragon to complete her cycle. If Sam didn't find a suitable mate, she would die unfulfilled and her spirit would cease to be reborn.

His captivity was now the least of his problems right now. He had to get out of here and fast. He began thinking that if he couldn't reach Sam, maybe he could call for someone else. He relaxed all his muscles, closed his eyes and began sending out his S.O.S. to anyone that could hear him.

Hawk was hit with a thought wave that felt like Tethys, so strong it nearly knocked him out of the air. He recovered and pumped his wings even harder. He began to feel more thoughts of distress, confusion and calls to battle. He listened and found that the entire supernatural world was in upheaval. Every being on this world that had the ability to communicate telepathically was being bombarded. Again, he pushed his wings all the more, trying desperately to reach the one person who could help get Justin and Max out of Mab's clutches.

Bataar, the unofficial king of Fairies and Mab's former general, consort, and the only real contender for her crown, was the only being to have ever survived an escape from Mab with his powers intact. Hawk had come across Bataar by accident a long time ago when he was just a young man. (Hawk wasn't exactly sure what his age was, but he had surmised that he was at least 1500 years old, piecing together fragments of memories with timelines.) Hawk had been lost, wandering the world looking for something, anything that would fill the emptiness inside him after his parents were killed. Hawk was the last descendent of a race of people the Navajo and Hopi Indians called Anasazi, or those who are not us, and were worshipped as spirit guides. The race of

Hawk people were called Thunder Hawks. With wingspans similar to a biplane, they had quite a frightening effect in their hawk forms.

He had been hunting in the Himalayan Mountains and spotted a juicy reptilian on the ground near a mountain stream. Making a dive for it, he suddenly found himself the captive instead of the hunter. Somehow, what he had interrupted was a birthing of a Chinese water dragon spirit. Whatever had grabbed him, had snatched him right out of the air a mere second before he reached the reptile with his talons. One second he was anticipating a nice lunch and the next he was lying face down. Wings, arms and legs bound behind him, trussed up like a turkey at Thanksgiving.

Once the birthing was finished, the beings dissolved into mist and his captor turned his attention back to his captive. "So, young hawkling, what have you to say for interrupting the ancient Chinese ritual of the birth of a water dragon spirit?"

Hawk remembered his times with Bataar fondly. The man had taught him a great deal over the years including how to defend himself in his human form. Other than MaMere, there was no one he trusted more. Bataar would help him find a way. He was sure of it.

Jamie came walking down the path to the house and when she emerged from the trees she found the place becoming increasingly crowded. People or beings were coming out of the woodwork... and some literally were coming out of the timber of the trees. Armed to the teeth and ready for battle.

Aundrea was standing on the porch trying to keep everyone from storming the house in response to an S.O.S from Tethys. Jamie had to get to the porch and explain the situation. She would have to get in the water in order to get around them, for they were packed in so thick, she didn't think she would get through.

As soon as Jamie came near the shoreline, she was nearly dragged under the water by Splash. Splash squeezed Jamie close to her, looked around to make sure no one was watching them and looked Jamie in the eye and said, "Someone told me Lizard Boy is being held prisoner. Is this true?" Jamie stammered and told her what had happened and then asked, "Why does it concern you? I thought you hated him.

I expected that this would make you happy, that there was a strong chance you would get your wish and he would be out of your hair permanently." Splash avoided the question, "Tell me where the Sidhe is." Jamie told her she wasn't sure of the exact coordinates, but Jace had just come from there. From what she could tell it was near the outskirts of Deridder, about a mile northeast of Lake Bundic.

Splash then pulled her closer, "Conjure me scuba tanks filled with sea water, now! I know you can do it with Tethys's staff." Jamie stepped back from her, "Ummm... I don't know if that's such a good idea. I have already set my pants on fire trying to conjure a ball gown like Cinderella's to practice. You could get hurt if I tried."

Splash kicked at the water, "You have to try! No one will expect a Nereid to attempt the rescue, so Mab won't be on the alert for water creatures! I am the only one that can slip under her radar!" Jamie looked at Splash a little harder and laughed, "You're in love with him. All the fuss and dramatics you created...why? Besides, Hawk said not to do anything till he gets back."

Splash screamed, "I don't give a

snail squirt what Featherhead said, I'm the only one that can pull this off!" Jamie kept staring at her with an ummmhmmm look, "Featherhead huh, isn't that Max's catch phrase for Hawk?"

Splash, unable to deny it any longer, looked down at the water lapping at their legs, "When I first laid eyes on him, something clicked, but we were of two different races. Not that it is all that big of an issue in our world, but I have a responsibility to mate with someone who will become heir to my mother's throne. I tried to suppress my feelings based on my responsibilities, but then he kept coming around, teasing me at first. Then he began to turn my own people against me, making me look like a heartless tyrant. I was furious with him." She looked up at Jamie again, "I just can't let him die like this without telling him how I really feel."

Jamie looked at her, gave her a hug and said, "Even if I could get you the gear, how in the world are you going to get there, or have you forgotten you don't have legs?" Splash looked hard at Jamie and whispered in her mind, "You know the little mermaid stories... well, they aren't all Hollywood fantasy. At birth we are granted a wish of love. We only have the one and it can never be reversed." Jamie's eyes widened, "You're not going to wish for legs are you?" Splash smiled and said, "Not exactly...Since I met Max, I have had time to think about it and I have something a little more inventive in mind that will still allow me to be a Nereid."

Jamie looked at her a moment longer, "Ok, stand back... just in case." Jamie gripped the staff, closed her eyes and concentrated on visualizing what it was she needed. A double set of tanks with all the apparatus appeared for a moment and promptly exploded. Jamie and Splash surfaced on the water and Jamie asked, "Too much water pressure in the tanks?"

Now they had everyone's undivided attention with the noise of the explosion. Aundrea parted the crowd like Moses at the Red Sea and asked what the hell she was doing at a time like this. Jamie explained what she needed and Aundrea smacked her forehead with her hand and started cussing in French. She stomped off to the storage shed and came back a moment later with scuba gear and threw it at them. She directed her ire at Splash, "If you had been paying attention to your sister, you would know that several of your wogs have been joining Maddey and Adey on adventures here on land, so MaMere had these made so they could all play together in the water and on land!"

Both Jamie and Splash looked a little sheepish. Jamie handed Splash her bowie knife and the gear and said, "Send me a mind link only if you get into trouble. Mab may be monitoring everything including the air close to her Sidhe. I know I would if I were in her shoes." Splash nodded, took the gear and disappeared in a dive under the water.

Jamie turned back to Aundrea and began to trudge out of the water to the porch when she noticed Lucky and his Clowder was standing off to the side of the house. She nodded her head at him to follow her to the porch for support.

Jamie mounted the steps to the porch. She hated speaking in front of large groups like this. They were milling about allies and enemies in the same small area in an extremely agitated state; some yelling about danger and wars.

17 GENERAL JAMIE IN COMMAND

If she didn't straighten this out this would get real ugly really fast. She tried to tell them to calm down so she could be heard, but the harder she tried the louder they got, some of the older beings calling for Tethys, younger, more local groups demanding MaMere/Stella.

Jamie looked out at the crowd and back at Lucky. He looked her with a smirk and a shrug and said, "Chere, ya always tellin Hawk and Stella dat you is capable of handlin yaself. Now is de tahm to prove it, yeah. And remember, if dey smell fear, dey will eat you alive...literally."

Jamie turned back to the crowd, straightened her shoulders and banged the end of the staff on the floor of the porch. The sound the staff made was more like thunder, but she held her ground and waited for them to quiet down.

Never batting an eye, she began, "Thank you for answering MY call. I'm sure that you are aware by now that Tethys or MaMere, Stella for those of you not familiar with her identities, is indisposed at the moment." More murmurings began in the crowd again and she continued, "I assure you she is safe and is en-route back here. In the meantime, she has entrusted me to handle this and all other matters in her stead until she returns."

Jamie paced the porch in a posture of strength, looking at many in what she assumed were their eyes to assert her meaning, "With Tethys unavailable, a situation has arisen that may put all clans and races in danger. Mab has awakened."

Now you could have heard a pin drop on the mainland. "From our reports, she intends to ascend to the surface and feed on the new magic that now exists. She has also captured one of our newly discovered dragons to amplify those powers."

For effect she let her sentence hang for a few seconds before continuing. "As you all know, Mab, fully charged, is a dangerous and unpredictable force. It is not known if she intends to cohabitate under our current treaties and alliances or if she intends to pursue a more dominant role topside. However, her past history tells us that during her reign as queen of Faerie, she could be kind and benevolent one moment and volatile the next. To put it in more modern terms, she is the epitome of a bi-polar schizophrenic with superhuman 'roid rage. Unpredictable is a very kind word to describe her."

"In any event, we need to organize and assume the worst as to not be unprepared and caught unawares. Since I am not familiar with all your abilities and political issues, I urge you to put aside your differences in a united effort for the good of us all. Number one:

please send one leader of each group to the front of the yard, number two: separate yourself based on the similarities of your strengths so we may utilize your services effectively. Number three: When you have sorted yourselves, send your leaders to me at the big table and be prepared to list your strengths to me quickly and we will begin our strategy of defense and offense."

Jamie turned to go back into the house and Lucky and Aundrea fell in behind her. Lucky patted her on the back and said, "Well done. MaMere chose a worthy general. Hawk will be proud." Jamie snorted, "Yeah right, that's because the shit hasn't hit the fan yet. I'm bluffing, hoping for more time." Lucky said, "Like Ah said Chere, well done. Play to your strengths and theirs. Making hasty decisions without intel results in dead troops."

Jamie turned to him as she entered the dining room and assumed the place at the head of the table, "Well said, Lieutenant Lucky, you're hired. Where did you get your military training anyway?" Lucky realized he was stuck and sighed his capitulation, "I have served in several military operations over the last couple of centuries. My experience includes: leading my band of mercenaries on a special ops team in volatile search and capture missions in Desert Storm and 2011 Yemeni al-Queda crackdown, The Cambodian/Thai border dispute of 2008, The Dissident Irish Campaign, The Islamic insurgency in the Philippines, World War II, World War I, The Civil War, The War of 1812 – I fought in the Creek War and the Chickamauga Wars in 1776."

Any normal person would be shocked and astounded at this military resume, but to her, this was actually just a quick rundown of recent events. In the grand scheme of things, Lucky wasn't that much older than she was by only a century or two.

Jamie nodded at his report and asked, "How many men do you have and what are their strengths and natures?" Lucky started to respond when Scratchy made him stumble as he took a step toward the table. "Would you PLEASE get your damn cat away from me!?" She arrived with Aundrea and Sam two weeks ago and has attached herself to me like a tic on a bald hound dog! If I didn't know better, I would think she was in heat the way she has been displaying!"

Jamie looked at Scratchy Patchy and searched the little cat's mind, "What's up little girl? Why are you bothering our good friend Lucky? You have never left the island that I know of without MaMere, why now?" The little cat stalked up to Jamie and wound herself around her legs and replied on Jamie's link, "You have found a mate, Tethys has gone off to claim her mate, even the dragon has found hers but doesn't know it yet, so I have decided it was time I staked my own claim." Jamie bent down surprised, "You have chosen Lucky for your mate?" The little cat popped her tail and went back to curl around the man's legs again. "Yes, I am perfect for him. He is surrounded by feline brawn, a natural leader. The perfect match for one with such an agile mind and intellect as my own, purrrrrrfecction."

Jamie stood back up and put her hands in the air, "Right now I am a general, not a couples counselor, you're on your own." Lucky's eyes bugged out and he plopped down in the nearest chair, "Great, just what I needed right now. Is she aware that the other females in my Clowder are also in heat? At least she is too small to cause too much trouble with the other females." Jamie huffed, "I wouldn't relax too fast, and you weren't there during the Hell Storm when she took on some trolls and witches. Those little claws of hers are like titanium buzz saws and she moves faster than even my eyes can detect. You might want to remember pretty is only skin deep and bigger isn't always better. After all, she IS a Were-cat too."

Lucky raised an eyebrow and said, "No shit?" Jamie nodded. "No shit." He looked down at the little scruffy ball of fur now curled in his lap, "Mais yeah, Chere, you a fighter, you? Yeah, you might jest make a good molly for me after all." Jamie looked at the little cat's shining weird eyes and gave her a conspiratorial wink. Scratchy raised her chin, closed her eyes to contented slits and began to purr.

Jamie got the list of the members of Lucky's mercenaries. (They included three panthers, four cougars, two cheetahs, five lions and two tigers, one natural liger.) Lucky was a sabre tooth tiger himself. His ability to channel the prehistoric spirit was the one characteristic that attracted him to this area of an odd conglomeration of the last remaining prehistoric Were creatures on the planet. Though not really as old as prehistoric times, Were creatures, with incredibly strong spirits, were able to dig deep into their genetic frameworks.

After Lucky's troop tally was complete, she enlisted him together with Aundrea to finish getting the pertinent troop intel for assignment to the appropriate strategic plans. She appointed each leader as a company commander and left it up to them to complete their assigned operations.

The task was to deploy a recon mission that consisted of the two panthers for stealth and surveillance. Three gnomes were sent to gather Sidhe tunnel intel with Jace and Lynne for aerial support and recon; Jace in his Hawk form and Lynne in her falcon form. Both resisted at first, sticking to Hawk's mandate of keeping away until his return,but were coaxed into participation on the premise that Hawk would need this information as soon as possible on his return.

Jamie was left to gather the rest of the troops together into a formidable supernatural army that had never before in history come together to fight side by side for a common cause. There were a few disagreements and skirmishes, but with that staff in her hand, she felt power and confidence running through her veins like never before. She just hoped that all she had to do was hold it. If it came to a crucial moment and she had to actually use it, she was terrified to think what might happen.

She sat pouring over old historical accounts of wars, anything she could find on Mab and interrogated every Fae available that had ever seen her, to the point of being accused of having some involvement with the Gestapo.

What it all boiled down to was that Mab had terrified every Fae creature to the point that most would rather die than actually be in her presence. She ruled the Fae with an iron fist, treating most disputes and territorial issues with a frank and open fairness that could be harsh but effective. For instance, in the Bible, there is a story of King Solomon, who had a dispute over a child and his ruling was that the child would be cut down the middle and each mother would get her fair share of the child. The true mother quickly relinquished her claim on the child, rather than see it die, was given the child in the end, proving that only the true mother would make such a sacrifice. Mab used that same harsh logic in her dealings. So severe at times, that when it came to decide whether or not to bring an issue before her, both parties would rather withdraw. Punishments for the losing parties were much harsher than the solutions to the problems.

Jamie also found that Mab was a very jealous and vain creature, creating harsh punishments for any slight she might perceive. There was a vague report that she was keeping the daughter of one of her most trusted generals prisoner in her keep.

The daughter was Elvish and of age to find a mate. She kept the young girl chained and constantly stimulated to keep her alive, but unable to fulfill any of those needs. The constant strain would eventually kill the girl if she could not satisfy her needs. Another twist to this cruel situation is that Mab had also located the girl's intended mate, placed him drugged and chained near the girl and forced him to perform certain acts in front of his intended that humiliated and scorned him.

Mab was indeed a very dangerous woman. If you weren't very careful with every action, word and movement in her presence, she could interpret it anyway she wanted... for all eternity.

18 YAYYY PIRATES!!!

"Land ho!" I yelled. Jean came up from the cabin with a chart and spyglass in his hands. Raising the glass to his eye, he said, "Land ho?"

Still grinning like an idiot pleased that I was the one to spot it first, "Yeah, isn't that what sailors used to say when they spotted land on the horizon?" Jean lowered the spyglass, looked at his

charts and patted me on the back
laughing, "Mais oui, Mon Amie, that is
indeed what we used to say... a hundred
and fifty years ago!"

"Since when did you get modernized
and how?" I asked him. "Ohhh, you
knowww, I get around, yes? I listened
as people talk and they didn't even know
I was there. Haha! I had a long time to
listen, non?" I looked at him a few
minutes more and said, "The battery is
dead on my cell phone now ,isn't it?"

No sooner than the land became
completely visible, Jean spotted a boat
speeding toward us. Jean raised the
spyglass once again and spotted not one
but three boats loaded with men armed
with AK47's, two of which had machine
gun mounts. They were heading
straight for us.
Jean jumped into action, slamming
hatches closed, gathering weapons and
placing them all about the deck in
strategic places. He opened a hatch
near the bow of the ship, hauling on a
chain that must have been attached to
pulleys under the deck. A platform rose,
revealing a small cannon with shot and
powder stacked beside it. All the while
he was shouting instructions to me to
attend to the rigging, raise this sail,

lower that one, do this, do that.

As the boats came nearer, Jean began loading the cannon with a gleam in his eye and a maniacal grin on his face. Taken completely by surprise, the first shot rocked our ship with its force and nicked the bow of the closest boat, taking out one of the machine guns. Obviously taking them by surprise, they didn't think we would be armed. Now they did and began to return fire.

Well within firing distance now, shots were hitting our ship. Jean yelled for me to keep down and threw a rifle to me and told me to cover him while he reloaded the cannon. I have never laid eyes on a rifle this old before. As I shot my first shot and then pulled the trigger to fire again, nothing happened. He yelled, RELOAD! Finding bags of shot and powder in the little cubby holes in the railings of the deck, I put the shot in with the powder, hands shaking all the while. Praying that I did it right and wouldn't blow myself up, I took aim and shot again. Boom! I got it right.

A little more confident now, I began loading and aiming for the boat motors and hulls, hoping to sink them rather than kill them. Jean fired a shot from the cannon and sunk the other armed boat and he cursed at them with glee, "Yes! Manger de la merde et mourir asticots! Ha Ha!

The remaining two boats came in boarding range of our ship and Jean abandoned the cannon and took up a rifle and a pistol. Firing furiously, we decreased their numbers, but we were just unable to compete with automatic weapons. We held them at bay for about ten minutes when the first wave of pirates flooded our decks.

Unable to reload fast enough, Jean took up his swords and began cutting down any who got close. I suddenly realized that my swords were in the cabin. What an idiot! I began to fight using all the martial arts training I ever had.

I whirled, kicked, punched, flipped and dodged. I felt a burning pain in my shoulder, but ignored it. Then I felt my knee explode as a bullet took me down. I looked over to Jean and saw that he had taken several shots as well, but when he saw me go down, he bellowed in rage.

A roaring growl emitted from his throat, his eyes turning to green slit pupils, enlarging in his head. Stunned, the pirates paused in surprise. The deck began to vibrate and Jean roared louder and suddenly the whole ship was rocked as nearly two tons (or more) of Louisiana alligator was deposited on the deck.

Screaming in French terror, a few more shots rang out from the intruders and Jean began to clear the decks with his tail of the remaining men that had not been thrown overboard by the unbalanced ship. Catching one of the men with his surprising speed by the legs, he snatched him up and promptly ate him alive, whole and still screaming. That did it. Any remaining pirates were now gone.

To those not accustomed to seeing a gigantic alligator moving faster than lightning, it would be a nightmare they would never forget... That is, if they survived the encounter.

Seeing stars, I began to pass out from pain and blood loss. Fighting for consciousness, I experienced a blinding blow to my head from the inside. It was Jamie and she was in trouble. I sat up, panting with pain and looked at Jean who hissed and roared, getting the same message. I searched for Tethys with my mind and found her surprisingly near and reached out to her.

I sent the message to Jean; he calmed a little and came to me, wrapping his tail around me to hold me up in a sitting position while we waited for Tethys, growling his gator growl the whole time, guarding me.

19 A WITCH RIDING ON A KILLERS BACK

Tethys sped along in the ocean to find the man she loved - to either claim him or release him. She remembered the fun they had together. Always laughing, always content with each other... until he boarded that damned ship. He would be gone for months at a time with never a word sent or a thought spared for her.

She worried constantly that he would

be killed in those crazy escapades of his. She told him over and over that she could give him anything he wanted and that there was no need to go pirating.

He would only laugh and tell her that he was a man and it was HIS responsibility to provide and protect, not hers. He would never be a kept man. He said that a kept man is lazy and fat and becomes just like the greedy aristocrats that fed off other people's labors. He would never stoop so low.

She would counter argue that this was her island and he could provide for her just fine and in any fashion he chose right here. He would only shake his head and tell her that the sea was in his blood. To take the rolling of a ship out from under his feet would be to cut his legs off and then what good would he be? Besides, he had his men to think about too. They had families to support as well. On and on it went with one argument after another, both refusing to give in to the other. He needed his independence, she worried for his safety. The only thing they could agree on was that while he was with her their love for each other was endless.

She shook her head at those memories. Realization can be a

humbling thing. The point was that they were both trying to protect and provide for each other in their own way. To survive, one of them was going to have to give in.

She knew that she would outlive him, so the compromise would be hers. She would do whatever she had to do to keep him as long as she could...even if it meant giving up her powers until he eventually perished.

The thought of his inevitable demise took her breath away and made her heart ache. She simply couldn't imagine living without him, no matter what form he was in.

So deep in her own thoughts she didn't notice the water getting quite so rough or the skies darkening until she was slapped in the face by a wave and the onslaught of pelting rain. She looked toward the horizon and saw a familiar countenance coming toward her, her daughter, Calypso.

Calypso's ghostly form floated over the whitecaps, coming nearer. "Mother, grandmother, Tethys, MaMere, Stella and whatever other monikers you might claim." She slightly bowed in respect. "What brings you into my realm of dream and storms?"

Tethys slowed the whales so that they could talk. "Calypso, why have you not revealed yourself to me before now? I had thought that you were gone from this existence with the others." Calypso laughed with the sound of splashing water, "My physical form has gone, but when the others started fading away, I poured my essence into the seas. I can manifest this form when the waters are infused with energy, as they are now."

Tethys nodded her understanding, "There have been many storms, daughter, why have you not come to me before? I have always loved you even when you were at your worst, as is the nature of who I am." "Dear Mother, you have made a deal with Him for your existence. The others on this side of reality are jealous of you and resent your being allowed to remain with powers intact. There were so many stripped of those powers and left to remain as human, defenseless as babes among wolves."

Tethys replied, "My power was never of a violent nature. There is so much about me that was already part of His purpose; it was only a natural course of events that I follow Him."

Calypso turned and kicked at the

water in her frustration, "Yet you remain with your powers! You are not a goddess if you follow Him! For that, dear Mother, I will keep you from the man you love. You will also pay for helping The Mariner who destroyed my lover! Tit for tat!"

"Calypso, don't be silly. You know as well as I do when the Lord, God, awakened from his rest, all of us were doomed. He is all powerful and much more than we ever were. Our powers only came into being when humans, ignorant or too greedy to abide by his sanctions began to believe and invent us in their minds. When they quit believing, we perished. As for your old lover, YOU created the situation and that man chose to save his fellow sailors over turning to you. Not only did your lover suffer, but you also managed to get another man condemned for all eternity for destroying what he thought was a bad omen. You have inadvertently managed to help create a plague on this earth in your petulance. It is your own jealousy that caused the whole thing and you know it! Admit your fault or be banned from this existence in any form!"

Calypso yearned for the companionship of her mother, and

thought over her response carefully. In her own way, she capitulated by offering a challenge to Tethys that would keep her pride intact. "Well countered, dear Mother. However, for your participation in my affairs in helping The Mariner who killed my lover, you must survive this storm to reach your own love. I am allowed this small form of revenge for your interference."

Tethys nodded, knowing that to resist might result in Calypso focusing her vengeance on Jean instead, so she braced herself. The storm became a hurricane and Calypso dissolved on a wave of her own delight. Tethys communicated to Asia and Phoros that they needed to dive and travel under the storms as much as possible. Tethys tethered herself to the killer whales with the items that Jamie had fortunately put in her long braids.

She gave the whales a signal to where her last impressions of Jean were and told them she was going to make herself go into a trance to be able to survive without oxygen. She wasn't sure how long it would last, so she told them to not waste a second getting to the goal. If she survived this test, not only would she be free, but that would also bind Calypso from harming Jean in any way forever.

With the water raging, Tethys closed her eyes and expelled her last breath to induce the trance that would save her life and help her reach her goal.

The whales dove with their precious cargo deep beneath the waves. Mates for life, they understood the devotion and need to be together, for they were not your average whales. Protected and gifted with immortality by Poseidon, for heroic deeds during battle, they had seen a great many things. This would be one of their greatest tasks yet.

Tethys dreamed and flowed with the currents of water speeding her along. She dreamed of the old days, of friends, long dead humans and old Gods lost to oblivion. She dreamed of new friends, new lovers, her new life and how much more it meant to her.

Tethys, happy in her dreams, was suddenly jolted by a strong pressure for her to wake, to return, for help. She responded not by waking, but by reaching out with her thoughts to assess the situation. Touching minds closest to her own, she began to create a sort of mind communication chain back to Jamie.

The storm was suddenly behind her and the whales were nearing the surface of the waters once more for their own air when she began to rouse herself out of her trance. Lungs bursting for air, she screamed and gulped, desperate for the precious oxygen that was a habit assumed for appearances only the day before.

It was dark and moonlight highlighted the water. She called for her daughter to appear. Calypso appeared in a foggy mist, a summoning she could not refuse.

"You survived. I underestimated your abilities in that human form." Tethys, still breathless, wiped the hair out of her face and adjusted herself into a sitting position on the back of Asia and said, "Calypso, one of the reasons you could never have survived in your physical form is that you were always so greedy and adamant in your own needs, that you often forgot the needs of others, no matter how small. Seeing to those needs and providing a helping hand once in a while, creates lasting friendships. One of the things that I have learned is that you can survive a great many things if you have strong friends to help you! Now! I banish you by right of this victory from ever harming me or mine in any way for as long as we live."

Calypso narrowed her eyes and turned away and thought about what her mother said. She turned, bowed again and replied, "Well done, once again you have outwitted me, even as a human. I will heed your words and honor your victory. I have been thought of as impetuous and incapable of reason in the past. I, too, have learned a great many things in my time as a spirit of storms. I will grant you a boon of a speedy current to carry you to your goal. My revenge has been satisfied once and for all." The fog began to dissolve and float away.

Tethys, surprised at the depth of feeling in her daughter's words, began to feel the currents pulling her and her companions. She turned into the direction of the currents and heard one last murmur as she sped off on her journey, "I always loved you too, Mother."

Tethys' eyes teared at the speed of their travel making it hard to see, but she persevered with one goal in mind, to reach Jean. She first spotted that cursed ship of his on the horizon and she thought that it was the first time she was actually glad to see it. She began sending out messages on her thought chain. Apparently, the whole damned world was in uproar. She had only been gone for three days and everything had turned to crap. Couldn't she ever catch a break?

20 REUNITED AT LAST

Tethys climbed a rope left dangling over the side of the ship to climb over the rails. Surprised that she found Jean back in his alligator form, she was hesitant as she stepped over the edge, wondering what had happened.

Dan was unconscious from blood loss and pain, but his pulse was still steady. Dan possessed an inner strength few suspected but her. She looked toward Jean and sent him her thoughts.

"I came to confess my crimes to you and hope that will forgive me." Jean hissed and circled her feet and flopped on the ground looking at Dan. "Oh, all right, it can wait, but I need your help. In order to make this crazy trip, I had to give my powers to Jamie and leave her in charge, so I need you to concentrate on what I'm about to tell you." Jean grunted and swished his tail once more.

"Jean, I hate to admit this, but you have always been the one in control of your form. I only cursed you to change forms when you were enraged. If you calm down, relax and think of pleasant memories, you will be a man again. You have actually done it plenty of times. Remember when Lynne came flying in and asked about the man I was talking to on the beach?" Jean grunted, "Well, that was you! You had been taking a nap and I walked up and found you there in the buff and enjoyed the sight, so I let you stay that way a little while longer. When she asked about the man, your jealousy returned and you sprouted four legs."

Jean stalked up and down the deck a few times, slamming the rails with his tail as he went. When he finally stopped in front of Tethys again, he stared at her and turned to look at Dan who was turning grey.

He settled down next to Dan and Tethys knelt beside him and stroked his hide a little. After a few minutes, Jean's breathing calmed and he changed back again. Naked, but no longer wounded, he reached over and pulled Tethys across Dan with surprising strength and kissed her hard. Then he turned her over lifted her little skirt and spanked her... hard. She screamed at him that this was doing Dan no good at all and they were wasting time.

He released her and said, "Ok what do I need to do? Tethys, still rubbing her butt replied with a glare, "I am going to give him what strength I have, but I will probably pass out after that. I need you to tell Dan to call for Asia and Phoros and any others that can help, that we need to get back to Old Lady Lake pronto! All Hell has let loose and Mab is awake." Jean nodded, "Who's Mab?" Frustrated, Tethys said, "I'll explain later, but it's not good. You can also tell Dan to call for Calypso. She may or may not help, but it's worth a shot."

"Calypso? I thought she was dead with the others?" Tethys gave him another exasperated look and laid her hands on Dan's wounds and closed her eyes.

Dan began to stir a little and all the color in Tethys face drained away slowly. Dan moaned and Tethys pushed harder, healing him slowly. It took quite a long time, but by the time Dan's eyes opened, Tethys was losing consciousness.

Jean did his part and explained the situation quickly to Dan while he gathered Tethys in his arms and took her to his cabin.

I felt a little worse for wear, a little sore in places, but my mind was on Mountain Dew and I felt like he could talk with the molecules if he wanted. Tethys had given me her own strength. The remaining strength of a Goddess and it packed a wallop for a human.

I reached out to touch Jamie's mind and she made me aware of all that was going on. The situation was this in a nutshell; Mab, Evil Queen of the Faerie, was awake and looking to install her own new world order; Max and Justin had somehow ended up as her hostages; Sam was in season(?) and would somehow die soon if she didn't get what she needed (Lord help the poor guy chosen for that duty).

Hawk had taken off to gather reinforcements to parts unknown; Splash was off on her own rescue mission with scuba tanks and her life's wish to save Max; Scratchy has a crush on Lucky; Aundrea, Lucky, Lynne, Jace and a few others had just been sent on a recon mission to scout for intel on the bad guy, oops, sorry...queen, and last but not least, Jamie fried her best pair of boots with Tethys' staff and inadvertently set all the supernatural world at Defcon Five with her S.O.S call. Oh, and she's sorry she got the wrong idea about me leaving.

Yup, that pretty much sums up the situation. I sent her the details of our own predicament and she took a moment to ask about Tethys and Jean. I told her that I didn't know, because when I woke up, Jean was carrying Tethys to the cabin and I haven't seen them since, but I could sense that Tethys was ok, just exhausted and drained. I felt Jamie's relief and told her that I was going to try to do what Tethys had instructed, but wasn't quite sure how I was going to manage it.

Jamie got the crazy idea that we could use our mind link and channel Tethys's powers to get us back, but I nipped that one in the bud and told her "Didn't you just tell me you set your boots on fire and almost got the world in a war the last time you used the staff?"

Jamie, suddenly quiet, "Maybe you're right, but what are you going to do?" I thought about it for a moment and a plan began to form. "I will let you know in a little while if we need to go to plan b." I can't believe she fell for it and asked, "What's plan b?" I simply dropped the connection and continued to formulate my plan.

My first course of action was to follow Tethys's instructions, but I did it in a different way. I acted as a hub for thoughts instead of a link in the chain. I contacted Asia and Phoros and told them what I knew and asked them to contact others that could help. I sent a thought to Hawk and reached him, though I could tell he was very far away. My connection to him was faint, so I gave him the short version and asked him to do the same thing that I had asked of Asia and Phoros.

Not being used to other being's thought patterns or the correct way to "talk" to them, I didn't want to make the same mistake Jamie had and have everyone in an uproar again.

My plan began to work. Nereids and whales and a myriad of other sea creatures showed up and began to haul the boat. From what little I had already gleaned from Jean, I began to adjust the rigging into the wind to change our course. Being so close to land at the time, a few of the Nereids simply brought over the fresh water and foodstuffs we might need.

Everyone was anxious because of the passengers that the ship carried. It seemed as if the whole sea paced, waiting for Tethys to wake up and wave out her window.

We were moving along at a good clip when I began to think of Tethys other instructions. Being wary because of the tail of deception and revenge on the Mariner at Calypso's hand, I hesitated, not wanting to suffer his fate or one similar.

I called for Calypso. I got nothing. Then the small breeze that was filling our sales suddenly died down to nothing and the currents were holding the ship still, even with everyone pushing it along.

Calypso was here. I sent a message to everyone to back off and give us some space. I called again, this time a little more formally, "Calypso, daughter of Tethys, we request your assistance." I waited a few more minutes and nothing changed. I knew she was still present because the ship hadn't moved a millimeter. I waited...and waited....and waited.

Resigned that I may have just sealed our fates to those of the Mariner, I turned to go to the cabin to tell Jean what our new situation was and then I saw her.

She was beautiful and horrifying at the same time. She was mist or more like a hologram of a person. Like a ghost, she floated on the deck, her hair and clothing swaying in a nonexistent breeze. She had long dark hair of impossible length, not quite black, but the midnight blue of stormy seas. Her skin was the color of sea foam. Her eyes glowed like the moon and her figure was flawless in every way. She wore translucent clothing that looked like it was constructed of very thin seaweed leaves. Relieved, I bowed my head a little to her to acknowledge her presence and she smiled back at me.

She was absolutely gorgeous until she smiled. With that evil grin filled with very sharp sharks teeth and the light glowing in her eyes, she was terrifying. I had to swallow my stomach before I spoke.

"Thank you for answering my call Calypso. I am ignorant of the politics of conversing with goddesses and ask your indulgence for a human such as I." She raised one eyebrow and took a few steps (or floating steps) toward me, "Granted, Mr. Rawlings, I will address you in the modern terms of this time."

"Thank you again. I was instructed by your mother, Tethys, to contact you and ask your assistance to get us back to her home as quickly as possible. There is much at stake and your being a goddess, I am sure you already know."

She approached me closely and looked me up and down. She floated around me and I froze in place noticing the sharp talons on the end of her fingers. "That is where you are wrong Mr. Rawlings. Unfortunately, I am a goddess no more, but I thank you for acknowledging my past achievements. Nooo, now I am just a spirit of the sea and storms and currents." She kept floating all around me and lightly touching my hair and clothes with one of those nails. I am not aware of your situation unless you have spoken them

into the water. Please feel free to
enlighten me."

I swallowed, wondering what would be
safe for me to tell her and what would
not. I began carefully, "There is a
problem on land. Mab has awakened
and has taken some of our people
hostage. It appears she believes she
has been unfairly imprisoned and
intends to extract revenge, even though
the people who wronged her no longer
exist."

"I see," she said smiling. "That is a
bit of a problem. What do you think
needs to be done to rectify the
situation?" A little confused and even
more cautious, I replied honestly, "Well,
to most of us in this time, it shouldn't
matter where a person wants to live as
long as they don't harm others. So, if
she wants to be free, all she needed to
do was... uh, come topside and live
peacefully."

"In these modern times, the general
consensus is that we want to treat
others as we would like to be treated,
we work for a living, earning the respect
of our peers and giving them respect in
return. We do not believe in slavery of
any kind, we have laws that most
citizens abide and courts and a justice

system of our peers for those that break those laws."

"Holding others hostage and causing them harm for personal revenge goes against the laws that we believe in and it is my belief that Mab may be inadvertently breaking those laws."

She stopped her circling and floated over to the wheel of the ship to sit on top of it. "So, what you are telling me is that anyone can live any way they want to as long as it doesn't harm anyone else, is that correct?" I nodded and she continued, "And it doesn't matter who or what you are?"

Ok, here's where it was gonna get a little sticky to explain. "While the modern world has developed a system that allows everyone to have the right to flourish and prosper, they are not completely aware that beings such as you, Tethys, Jean or any other supernatural creatures actually exist. They are still under the illusion that the world contains only human and animal species. However, most individuals who have certain... special abilities do very well functioning in a human fashion, integrating into society. This allows for everyone to be treated equally, regardless of race or anything else. We live by these morals of God. No stealing, killing, hurting, deceiving or lying. Treat your spouse, children and parents with respect and be a good person. That is the code that most people and countries strive to achieve. There are still some that haven't quite achieved that conclusion yet, but for the most part the whole world works that way...regardless of religious beliefs."

"That's all very interesting, Mr. Rawlings. Thank you for bringing me up to date. What is it exactly that I can do for you to help you in your endeavor?"

"Actually, I would ask a very simple favor from you." She gave a short quiet giggle and my blood ran cold. "Be careful of how you use the term favor in the presence of creatures such as me. We tend to expect payment for those favors."

I thought about this for a moment and continued my request, "Should you grant us this favor, what would you expect in return?" She smiled wide and her eyes began to glow. She floated up to my face to look me squarely in the eyes. "I want you to talk to me every night. I want to hear about what is going on in the world; I want you to teach me what it is you humans want in life. I want you to tell me about your hopes and dreams; I want you to tell me about your loves and losses...for the rest of your life."

I didn't hesitate as she expected, "We have services that do that very thing. They are called newspapers. They contain stories not about just one person, but a whole city or world if you would like. They contain all the news and happenings that are going on in the world. They contain personal, political, human interest, legal and funny stories about our life as humans. I would be happy to get you as many subscriptions as your heart desires. After all, I am a journalist by profession. It is what I do to survive in this world."

Clearly I shocked her. She expected some devious haggling to avoid doing what she asked. She stared at me with a stunned expression and dropped her evil mask, "Really? You wouldn't mind? You would come to me every night and read them to me?" Uh oh, here is where I needed to think fast. "Not exactly, but I will do even better than that, I will teach you to read them yourself. After all, what will you do if something happens to me and I could no longer keep up my end of the bargain?" Again, she was stunned into silence. She paced, considering my terms.

While she thought about it, I began talking about the virtues of reading. "You know, learning to read is probably the most important thing you can accomplish. Think about it this way, most of the world's most important accomplishments are recorded in books. You can learn to do anything by reading a 'how-to book.' Hell, you might even get interested in writing your own book. Think of it this way, you could actually write in your own words the experiences of your life. What would that be worth to you?"

She suddenly stopped her pacing or floating back and forth. She looked up at me and said, "Anything, anything you want. Teach me to read and to write and I will do anything you ever ask."

It was my turn to chuckle. I just outsmarted Calypso! I told her, "I don't require anything but your friendship and your willingness to help on your own terms. I will teach you to read and write for free." Again, she was stunned. She floated up to me and put her arms around me and soaked me with mist or dew or something. "No one, no one has ever done anything for me for nothing."

She stood back and smiled, where should we begin? I smiled back at her and said, "We need to get this ship back to Old Lady Lake, like yesterday." She tapped her chin and looked back at me, "A few hours I can do, yesterday is out of the question. By the way, when I hugged you, you felt like my mother. Why?" I knew what she meant and didn't bother to correct her, "I was wounded by some pirates that tried to steal our ship. She healed me and gave me all her remaining strength. She is in the cabin, if you would like to check on her." She blinked, "Aren't you afraid I will try to kill her?" I looked her in the eye, "You are my friend and her own daughter. I trust that you would not betray either of us."

She nodded and started floating toward the cabin. "You might want to come with me; it might get a little windy out here." The ship lurched forward and the sails filled with a loud crack and I was nearly blown overboard. I struggled to keep up with her.

21 THE TINY SHIP WAS TOSSED

We went through some kind of tunnel with circling rings in it and the ship rattled and groaned under the velocity that we were travelling. Rigging was snapping all around me. Calypso had walked into the tiny cabin and Jean never took his eyes off Tethys. "You had better be friendly or I will kill you where you stand" he stated softly.

Calypso raised one eyebrow in response and replied, "She will be fine in just a few minutes, not that you could actually DO anything to me if she didn't wake but as soon as we get her back to her island and she picks up her staff, she will revive and be as strong as ever. Besides, I have a few interests to protect now. I am turning over a new leaf!" She floated over to the one remaining stool and smoked into a sitting position to wait, examining the interior of the little cabin.

Peeking out the porthole, I watched as we exited the tunnel and the turbulence stopped. I recognized a familiar landscape on the horizon and ran for the little door. The sun was shining and we were being carried to shore on a fast current. I went back into the cabin to give Jean an update and found that Calypso was gone. Tethys' eyes were open and the color was coming back into her face. Tethys smiled and asked where Calypso was and Jean told her that as soon as she began to wake, Calypso disappeared. Tethys coughed weakly, "That's a good thing. I just found out from the memories of the water that when she attacked me and I went under the water to escape her, you were actually riding out the storm above me! She is a wicked, wicked creature. She was trying to kill us both while we watched each other!"

Jean shushed her to keep her from wasting her valuable strength, "She seems to have changed her mind, and actually she is the one who brought us back to your island in time to save you." Tethys looked at him shocked and then stared off into the distance and muttered, "Well, it's about time. After all, technically I am still her mother."

Bubbles, Asia and Phoros were jumping in the waves. I lowered the platform that Jean and I had made for getting him in his alligator form onto the ship and was able to go down and "speak" with them about the progress of the situation.

Evidently, the only news that she could relay to me was that the island was inundated with supernatural creatures and Jamie appeared to have everything under control at the moment. A small dingy was brought out so that we could transport Tethys to shore.

Jean came out carrying her in his arms. He never let her go, even to get into the boat. Who needs motors or oars when you have a Nereid that can do twenty five knots without breaking a sweat? In no time we were wading through the surf to meet Jamie.

Staff in hand, she was more than happy to relinquish her command. The staff was laid in Tethys' arms and she glowed brightly for a minute or two and Jamie fell on her butt with the release of power.

Jean didn't want to put her down until she pushed at his chest and looked him in the eye and asked him if he wanted to grow scales again. He laughed and said, "Mi Amore, I could keep you in my arms forever and would never let you go if you would let me." Her eyes twinkled and she laughed back, "Time and place, time and place... now let me go, I have business to attend."

Jamie looked at Tethys and hung her head, "I'm sorry, as usual, you are coming to rescue me again." Tethys walked up to Jamie and put her finger under her chin to make Jamie look her in the eye, "You have absolutely nothing to be sorry for. I am not rescuing you; I am joining you in battle. You did very well and I am proud of you. In fact, if we get through this, I have more vacation plans in mind," she winked at

Jean and waggled her eyebrows.

Jean caught her meaning and began hustling everyone about, "We are wasting time! The battle is at hand, you heard the lady, allones!" Clapping his hands, he hurried everyone to the house.

I offered a hand to Jamie, as she was still sitting on the ground. She took my hand, smiled widely with that mischievous look she always had and came into my arms for a quick kiss. We might be at war, but right now everything was right in my world.

At the round table, we were all brought up to speed on where all of our troops were and what had been done up until now. She had not heard back yet from the recon party she had sent to investigate the situation at the Faerie Sidhe, but she expected them back at any time. No one had heard or seen anything from Splash.

Tethys had abandoned her old woman persona for the time being. She was studying a map of the waterways very closely to determine where they connected when she gave up frustrated and called for the Potomoi. We went outside to the little freshwater stream that ran through the swamp to the sea to meet with their leader.

Tethys spoke with him at length, finding out the best water route that she could take that would keep her within distance of the Sidhe and not lose her powers. It was a little tricky, but they found a way if the gnomes that were loyal to Tethys could burrow a passageway to join two streams together.

I asked Jamie what the importance of these streams meant. I told her that I knew she routinely went into town all the time and she explained that Tethys was bound to this island by her pact with God. As long as she was in brackish or fresh waters that mingled, she could travel outward from that point and when she went into town she never got more than five hundred feet from bayous that fed into the Gulf. The further she went the more her powers would weaken. She wouldn't die, but she would lose all powers other than physical strength that she was born with.

They were planning a route that would keep her in those merging streams to get her within striking distance of the Sidhe. There was only one point where one bayou came close to another but did not connect that was the issue. The gnomes would dig a tunnel and merge the two bodies of water.

I asked how she knew all this, because Tethys had only revealed herself as a goddess very recently. Jamie explained that when she was given Tethys powers, she was also given access to her memories and thoughts. I looked at Jamie with the realization that the transfer could have very well killed her with the magnitude of such a transfer of information, not to mention the power that went along with it.

I asked how she managed it and she said that Tethys did it very slowly, giving her mind time to expand and grow and her body to absorb and adjust. There were times when Tethys would have to withdraw a little to give Jamie more time, but in the end it worked.

My journalistic curiosity roused, I asked "If she was born, who was her mother? I thought she was one of the first Titans?" Jamie shook her head and said that she had wondered the same thing, but the memories of the birth of Calypso and some of the others explained it to her.

When the gods were born, they weren't born in a physical sense, but brought into existence from a merging of powers. Tethys was Poseidon's mother and wife in that when she was in the vicinity of his father, Poseidon was born and when she was in Poseidon's realm and her powers complemented his, Calypso came into existence. Jamie told me that when she was doing some research on Tethys, she always felt that part was a little creepy and incestuous. Now that the memories clarified the process, it was very similar to a chemical reaction rather than mating. Tethys essence is to nurture, hence her many, many 'children.'

Jamie snorted and said, "She is a regular fertile turtle." Tethys came up behind her and gave her a little push, "Very funny, I am glad you understand the birthing process. Would you care to emulate you, little turtle? I can arrange that, you know." Jamie swallowed her grin and choked on the visual image Tethys sent her of an old woman living in a shoe while lying on a bed, expelling children like ants in an anthill.

22 A DANGEROUS JOURNEY THROUGH CAJUN COUNTRY

Splash swam up the waterways as far as she could with the Potomoi prince she had enlisted as a guide. She was amazed that she could get even this close. When she first set out, she thought she would have to use her wish much earlier and travel overland by foot. This way was much faster and the saltwater in her tanks kept her surprisingly energized. Twice she had to teach an alligator a lesson about being a gracious host to visitors just passing through their territory, especially when they had teeth as sharp as her own.

She came to the point where she needed to cross over to another waterway to complete her journey. Getting the final directions and landmarks, she dismissed the prince and gathered her strength. She always thought her wish would be wasted as there was never anyone who even came close to capturing her attention. She had always been so busy governing her people, she considered love a weakness that would keep her from doing her job.

She concentrated and listened to the sound of the water all around her. She had thought very carefully about what creature she wanted to be. While there had only been rare cases of a Nereid using the Wish, they had always been used to change to a human, so she could be with the fisherman or seaman who had caught her heart.

Splash had better plans. The "Wish" was to transform her body to allow her to follow her heart. It never said that you had to transform completely or which form you had to take. She visualized her tailfin splitting into three limbs, similar to an amphibian with claws and webbing AND a new tail. Her arms would develop fins that would replace the power she lost from her large tail fin to move in water, very similar to that of a flying fish. With those simple adjustments, she would be able to continue her life as a modified Nereid and not give up the world she knew, but would be given access to the world above.

As she visualized her modifications, she made her wish. Her body convulsed in pain and magic. When it was over, she found herself lying half in, half out of the water. The modified scuba tank and regulator was badly damaged with the force of her convulsion and gnashing of teeth during her transformation. She started to gasp in panic at being without her saltwater breathing apparatus, but quickly realized that she could actually breathe in oxygen. She hadn't planned on it, but it was nice to know that her body had adapted lungs along with the other physical changes to allow her to become completely amphibious. Cool!

She gained her composure and her strength and concentrated on her next task, getting to the second waterway. She used her hands and gathered her new legs under her and crawled a few steps. She found her legs were stronger than she imagined and she fell on her face a few times until she could coordinate her movements, cursing the lack of time for a learning curve. She never realized how much balance played a key in human locomotion. She quickly found she could use the tail to help with her balance much like cats and kangaroos do to assist with balance and power.

She scanned the shoreline and calculated the shortest distance she would have to run to get to the water. There was a four lane road she would have to cross in order to reach it. Fortunately, there were trees on both sides to help conceal her, but nothing in between. She waited until she could hear no traffic sounds and she quickly made her dash to the other side. She had almost made it when she tripped over her own hind feet and whipped her tail in the wrong direction to compensate, lost her balance and fell face first onto the pavement.

She understood what Hawk's boys meant when they complained about road rash now; even her forehead was scraped by the asphalt. Thankful for her tough shark-like skin, there was little damage other than minor abrasions. She lay there for a minute trying to untangle herself when she heard a motor rumbling toward her. She panicked and stood quickly, took a step, lost her balance and fell again.

The truck's tires squealed and smoked as the driver slammed on his brakes to avoid hitting her. She used her hands and legs this time and quickly slithered to the safety of the trees. She turned and watched for a moment to see the driver and his passenger jump out of his truck and scramble to get a gun from the back of his truck and start running in her direction yelling, "It's de gawd-damned creature from de Black Lagoon! Git de gun, we gonna take dis one to de bank!"

She hissed in his direction and turned toward the water and in a giant leap from her powerful new legs she jumped high in the air and dove cleanly, disappearing into the dark waters of Bayou Black.

Panting at her close call, she took a moment to get her bearings, listening for sounds that the humans were in pursuit. They would surely be searching the area on a return trip. If Lizard Boy was still alive, then he could fly them out and she thought about dropping a parting gift on their heads.

Finding him alive, but what if he wasn't? She shook her head and told herself that there was nothing that could kill that stubborn dragon. She swam as fast as she could to get to her destination, repeating the directions over and over in her head to strengthen her resolve.

Lake Borgne to Lake Pontchartrain, Lake Pontchartrain to Bayou Black, Bayou Black to the Red River, Red River to Kisatchie National Forest, 1 mile due north to Grey Cemetery near a small lake.

Her contacts told her that there were small streams that fed that small lake. She would swim as far as she could and then rest in the lake and find a way in the Sidhe. She would wait for full nightfall before attempting any travel overland. Bad enough that there were going to be sentries guarding the place, but to attract any more human attention, especially after that last encounter, would be avoided at all costs.

Keeping her mind focused was the

only thing that kept her from losing it. She never imagined that she would have feelings this strong for anything. The thought of Max getting killed created a pain in her chest so strong she couldn't think straight. She was strong, the strongest of her kind. Not a silly female prone to bouts of weakness. She despised weakness in anything.

When she thought about it, that was probably the root of her attraction to Lizard Boy. No matter what she said to him or how badly she had treated him, he never gave up. Nothing ever seemed to faze him and very little seemed to hurt him. She admired that more than she cared to admit.

She was nearing the junction to the Red River when she realized that she was going to have to cross over another highway again to get to the right waterway. This highway was only a two lane road, but there was very little in the way of covering vegetation on either side for some distance.

Traffic was another problem. At this time of day vehicles used this route quite a bit. She would have to take a chance. This time, instead of standing upright, she hunched down and crawled like an alligator. In this area of

Louisiana, gators were a common occurrence and it was more likely that if anyone saw her, that at first glance they wouldn't think anything of just another gator by the side of the road or roaming along in the tall grasses.

Lowering herself to the height a gator would stand was a little hard and she had to again get her new legs coordinated for the effort. With her feet/back claws on the ground, she angled her knees outward and used her tail as more of a brace to support her upper body. Keeping her elbows tucked into her chest and just using her forearms for mobility, she thought she might just get away with it. Except for one tiny little detail….she was silver, not green or brown like an alligator.

She was just about to make the attempt anyway when a truck swerved and hit a mud puddle on the side of the road and slung mud and dirt all over her. Sputtering mad, she got up on her knees and looked at herself. Perfect! Now she was brown like mud, like an alligator, problem solved!

She began her crablike crawl across the road. Scrabbling as fast as she could, she cleared the road with no problem scooting into the grasses and disappearing into the landscape. She didn't wait around, but made good time in getting to the river. It was much further than she anticipated. By the time she slipped into the water, she was exhausted. Her new muscles screaming with the exertion of moving in a manner that they weren't designed to be used.

Relieved and taking a minute to catch her breath, she plunged on, swimming upstream against the current to the last leg of her journey. She swam for miles and miles, ducking boat propellers and the occasional fishing trawler working the river. Her new lungs gave her the ability to breathe on land. She could swim a long time underwater, but she was forced periodically to surface for air.

She saw the sign the Potomoi described that said Kisatchie National Forest. Not that she could actually read the sign but she was told it was right next to the old fallen oak tree on an old blue truck. From that point she knew that she would have to travel up an old drain pipe to a little stream that fed the lake near the Fairie mound.

It was full dark as she had expected, and the little stream she had to travel was just that, a little trickle of water down a rock bed. She barely had enough water to splash on her skin to keep it wet, much less actually swim in. She walked upright watching for any signs of humans or Fairie guards.

She reached the pond and could see the rolling hills in the distance. She sat and began to think of a way in. She began to play the game that Maddey and Adey loved so much. "What is the thing in this picture that does not belong?"

She began to look at the shape of the hills and then the shape of the landscape around them. For the most part, the land was flat with only a slight rise or bump on the landscape. Ok, that confirmed she was in the right place. Now to seek out an entrance. At first glance, she didn't see anything moving at all. Then she began to see that certain parts of the hillside kind of shimmered, the illusion at times not steady, revealing a small opening in the side of the hill.

Now that she knew where to look for the entrance, she knew there had to be other ways in and out. She began to think. If I lived in a hill, what are the accommodations I would need to survive? Oxygen, so a fresh air supply was essential. Water! I would need to have a fresh supply of water. Even under siege, I would need water! There had to be an underground source of water that led into the compound.

The nearest water supply was this little lake. She dove under the water to see if she could find a stream or tributary or hell, even a pipeline. She searched the bottom thoroughly and began searching the sides when she found an old rusted iron grating nearly covered over by weeds. A pipeline it was.

She pulled and tugged on it with no luck. Then she went in search of something to pry it off with. She tried a couple of tree branches, but they quickly broke. She needed something stronger.

She looked around the bottom and found an old boat anchor with a small amount of rope still attached. She wedged the anchor into the grating and pulled the rope to a tree near the bank.

Too short! Damn it! She popped her head above the surface and noticed an old farm tractor in the distance. Careful not to create an interesting silhouette, she did her gator crawl to the tractor. She searched all over the machine for something that might work and found a chain attached to some kind of other bladed equipment. She released the chain from the attachment and the tractor.

Tying the chain to the rope and then looping the chain around the tree and a piece of old stump, she was able to use a tree branch to pull her contraption tight and add more leverage to the anchor. She pushed and struggled and puffed. The grate had obviously been sealed by the one of Mab's minions; it still wouldn't budge.

About that time she saw two beams of light approaching the lake. A car was coming. She hunkered down, cursing her luck now that she had to wait until the humans left before she could go any further. She watched and waited.

It was a young couple. They had parked their old battered truck and were sitting there listening to the radio. Then they started kissing and groping each other. Terrific! This lake was the local make-out spot!

Fuming, she sat there waiting and then an idea came to her. She re-rigged her chain and rope looping it around another tree near the young couple's car. Then she snuck right up to the truck crawling the whole way and carefully looped it to the rear axle of the truck. She backed out from under the truck and slunk back into the water.

She started thrashing and making grunting and growling noises. By the time they started hearing the noises, she was really mad and the growling wasn't a bit faked. It sure took them long enough to notice!

They began looking out at the lake to see what was causing the noise. She began to thrash some more in the water. Then, when she was sure they were watching, she began to slowly rise upright from the water toward them.

She got waist high out of the water before they began to react and turned the headlights of the truck on to see her better. She raised her arms and spread her fins and claws. They began to scream in terror. The young boy, fumbling with the keys, tried to start the truck. In his fright, he forgot to engage the clutch, so it stalled several times before the engine roared into life.

It was still taking too long. She needed to really scare them and make them take off in a hurry. She began to use her new legs, praying she had gotten the hang of it to make a run at them. Pumping hard, she ran and howled her hardest.

The boy slammed the truck in reverse about the same moment the girl fired a shot. Those damned Cajuns! Did every single one of them have a gun in the window?! The shot went wild and she began to run in a haphazard pattern, decreasing her chances of actually getting shot. That part wasn't all that hard because she was struggling to maintain her balance and still run.

The boy turned the truck around just in time for her to bang on the bed of the truck. Another shot and the girl blew the back window of the truck out. Glass flew everywhere and she ducked her head, wincing as she felt the slice in her arm.

She quickly rolled on the ground, getting clear of the chain. The boy put the truck in gear and spun tires and mud when he punched the gas. The truck leapt forward, snapping the chain taut, and pulled the axle right out from under the truck to a dead stop.

The impact of the sudden stop had flung the couple forward. The boy, now unconscious at the wheel, the girl moaning and semi-conscious with a gash on her forehead, having smashed her face on the windshield.

Splash ran back to the water and dove

to the grate. It was still intact, but the impact had pulled one side of it loose. She squeezed her body through the opening and was on her way down the tunnel to the Sidhe. Heart beating a million miles an hour, she realized she had accomplished the impossible. A Nereid had infiltrated a Fairie Sidhe!

23 A MASQUERADING ARMY

Tethys in the lead, dressed in full battle armor, floated her army right up the bayous, waving to the crowds that gathered. Onlookers, used to celebrations and costumes in this area, thought that it must be a procession of Halloween masquerade revelers. They were greeted everywhere with cheers and merriment.

The company of Weres, also in full warrior form, were mistaken for humans in elaborate Halloween costumes. There were Lucky's Clowder of big cats, werewolves, gnomes, agogwe, bergrisar, eserinis, and even some of the more elusive creatures, rarely ever seen in daylight. They were all greeted with awe and admiration in the form of shouts and applause.

Sam, having recovered somewhat from her... illness, was determined and ready to fight and was another cause of great excitement in her half human form and breathing fire and smoke. Still unable to complete a full change, she still sported her tail, clawed feet, dragon eyes and teeth. She threw candy and beaded necklaces to the crowds.

The barges were decorated with all sorts of adornments. Tethys had decided that moving such a large contingent of supernatural creatures secretly over land to the Fairie Sidhe would be too risky no matter how stealthy they were.

It was Lucky's idea actually. After planning their route so that Tethys would be able to keep her power, we discovered that the route would take them into public view in many places.

Everyone was brainstorming to find a way to keep everyone hidden and stick to the only route that would protect Tethys. Frustrated, he stomped around yelling that we might as well just parade everyone right through the towns like a bunch of trick-or-treaters.

Jamie, hearing his grumbles, looked at Tethys and said, "Why not? If this place was ever famous for anything, it is their willingness to have a party! Why not have everyone shift forms and throw them candy and trinkets like they were in a parade. A masquerade procession!"

Tethys smiled, 'It might just work!" They gathered their troops and put everyone to work decking out the boats.

Some of the larger flying creatures wore harnesses that appeared to be attached to the boats, to look like they were kites or elaborate ballooned creatures.

Tethys was nervous with having so many different creatures compiled together. Some races had long standing feuds with others. There were races of creatures that fed exclusively on other creatures. Now they were all united for a common cause.

Sure, there were grumblings and scattered brawls, but for the most part, they all focused on survival. To continue to exist without interference in territories that some had fought almost to extinction to preserve.

With Mab's awakening and plans to take over the surface for a new power structuring, it would change everything all these people had fought so long and hard for. Then there was another factor, Mab took or stole magic from others to increase her own power. Given the chance and the availability of so much power for the taking, she could make living on the surface of this planet quite literally Hell on Earth.

The Gnomes had completed digging the links to the waterways. When it became apparent that they would have to abandon the boats and travel by land, they simply moved to the appropriated Mardi Gras floats and continued on to their final destination.

Once they arrived at Kisatchie National Forest, tents were quickly erected to house the private masquerade ball attendees. Any human officials that dared to question the procession were quickly dealt with either by simply 'changing their minds' or by a delicate restraint and a little 'time out" that only left a mild bump on the head.

As they approached the forest, you could really feel the magic in the very air. Mab was indeed awake and quite aware that Tethys was close. The scouting party had returned. There were small, hidden entrances to the underground fortress, but they were heavily guarded with magical alarms or by the Fae creatures.

The gnomes, again proving to be an invaluable asset, began digging new ways into the Sidhe all around the area. More troops were still arriving. Lucky, Jamie and Dan had their hands full, communicating commands and strategies either through telepathic thought or simple sign language.

Tethys had surrounded the entire area with her army. So far there was no sign whatsoever of Mab. It was eerily quiet to have such a large gathering of bodies in one area.

Lucky's idea to use human SWAT tactics and bombard the Sidhe with tear gas and hand grenades was a bit extreme, but would be considered if the hostages were not released.

The Fairie Sidhe and Mab's fortress was under siege for the first time in ...well, ever. No one has ever had enough power or reason to challenge

Mab.

Tethys paced back and forth in front of the main masquerade pavilion. Her combat gear looked like a sexy Halloween costume but was, in actuality, fully functional and lethal. As she turned in her pacing, her long braids would whip about her like flying knives. There were many razor-sharp blades and weapons implanted in those braids.

Jamie was quite pleased at the look Tethys presented in her new gear. (A person would wonder at the fact that sharp implements of death excited your girlfriend and be extra cautious to have on body armor when delivering any kind of bad news... note to self.)

Being as accustomed to Tethys' persona of MaMere as we all were, her new look brought home the fact that Tethys was a goddess. She had the power to not only kill, but devastate and annihilate if she so chose. The fact that she catered to her nurturing instincts for so long was a testament to her devotion to God and humanity.

As we watched her pace, we waited for her decision to attack. It was now well past noon on our first day of encampment. We all kept wondering what she had been waiting for, when a large shadow appeared overhead and an ear-splitting shriek; A hawk's call to battle.

Hawk landed and deposited another man on the ground who had been riding between Hawk's wings. He was a small man, very powerfully built with black hair, an Asian look to his features and a thin mustache that trailed down his chin almost to his chest.

He wore a helmet, but had a high que of hair from the top of his head that trailed down his back, with the rest of his hair that stuck out of his armor and grew to his boots. Those boots had the curling tips and would be kind of cute if not for the fact that the curved tip consisted of a sharp spike that looked suspiciously like a dragon's tooth. On closer inspection, most of the spikes on his armor looked like teeth...big teeth... and he was covered in them.

I quickly realized he was dressed in ancient Mongolian battle gear, complete with a bow strapped across his back and deadly looking curved blades at his waist.

Mongolians were traditionally raised much like the Spartans, who were also expert archers on horseback and ruthlessly cunning in combat. Mongolian warriors favored the scimitar for blade work. To this day, there are parts of Russia that the military will not enter due to the reputation of the Mongolians. When you think about Mongolians, you might visualize about a thousand angry little Conans with attitude. This is the very reason Genghis Kahn was so feared in his day. If not for the pointy ears, this man could have been mistaken for Kahn himself.

Hawk, having finished his change back to a human, introduced the little man, "Tethys, this is General Bataar, King of the Elves, and one-time consort and prisoner of Mab. Next to Mab, this man is the rightful ruler of all Fairie.

He is also the only being that has ever escaped her clutches and survived. Mab has destroyed or slaughtered his entire family with the exception of his beautiful daughter. To this day, Mab still has her imprisoned within her lair, torturing her on a daily basis. Bataar has made several rescue attempts to retrieve her, but without enough support, his efforts have been futile.

Tethys nodded her head and addressed him formally, "General Bataar, I have heard of your deeds and respect your knowledge and experience.

I welcome you as an ally."

In a deep, gravelly voice filled with the experience only centuries of wisdom and survival can produce, surprising for a man of such small stature and youthful appearance. He replied eloquently and precisely, "Tethys, Titan goddess of nurturing and motherhood, Mes Amie, MaMere Eschte, I have also been aware of your good deeds over time.. I am at your service, now and forever." Then he bowed, at the waist, never bending a knee - showing authority, but holding the controlled bow, eyes on the ground, acknowledging and giving respect and trust.

Everyone was quiet a moment as Tethys paid respect in turn, until Bataar had resumed his upright position and returned his eyes to her face. She took two strides forward, wrapped her arm around his shoulder and guided him into the tent to begin discussing tactics.

Bataar was very instrumental to our strategy. His knowledge of how the Sidhe is set up was invaluable. There are a series of tunnels that are more like a maze with dead ends and traps. He let us know where we should be able to find the triggers for the traps, so we could deactivate them and move forward.

Mab's central room or throne room, if you will, is at the heart of the maze of tunnels. Depending on how the Sidhe is currently situated, there will be a prison or torture chamber off to her left. There are also escape tunnels that she can use, behind and to the right of her seat, in the floor and one directly above.

All tunnels have traps, all tunnels are warded, but due to the ever constant changing nature of a Sidhe, some tunnels are not often checked and have been forgotten over time. Some have caved in and some have been unused for so long their magical alarms have disintegrated. The Fairie Sidhe is much larger than it appears and there is always a way from an old Sidhe site to a new one as a precaution in the event of attack. Since there was no one who has ever dared attack, these tunnels are rarely ever closed off any more.

Bataar went on to explain that no one knows how the tunnels are built. When the Sidhe moves, Mab tells everyone that it is time to move and then leads everyone and everything to the new site. Some sites have been changed due to the availability of fresh water or food, earthquakes, changes in the terrain or changes in the lines of magic, or Ley Lines, as they are sometimes called. Sometimes she moves just because she is bored.

He suggested that we retreat just a bit and look for signs of the connecting tunnel as a way to move more troops in at one time. Hawk asked if that might be more of a trap than anything. Bataar looked up and said, "And you don't think she hears the digging you are already doing and isn't prepared?" Hawk looked at Tethys and she nodded and commanded the messenger to contact the gnomes to tell them to stop digging.

Bataar stopped her, "Better yet, tell them to keep digging, just don't make any progress. She will continue to hear them scratching on her walls. We can keep her distracted thinking that we still plan to enter in that manner." Tethys looked at the messenger and nodded to accept the change in her order.

We continued to discuss tactics when Sam walked into the tent. She started to say something to Jamie when she stopped in her tracks, her mouth still open, her words frozen on her tongue and slowly turned to face Bataar standing opposite Jamie.

She blinked and walked toward him.

When she was standing directly in front of him he smiled, "It has been a long time since I have laid eyes on one of your kind. You are troubled? Here, let me help." With that, he reached out his hand and put it on her chest, over her heart, and cupped her cheek with his other hand. She closed her eyes and exhaled, nuzzling him and moving to lay her head on his shoulder for an embrace.

Hawk, ever vigilant, said, "She has found her mate. Bataar is also known as brother to dragons. He nurtures, heals and cares for other dragon species. His blood sings to theirs in a harmonic balance. He has also been searching for another mate since his first wife died in Mab's prisons. Starved of love, attention, and space to move...she was a wind dragon.

24 A LIFE FOR LIFE

Everything was quiet. Not even cicadas were chirping. Jace and Cecile had been chosen to bodyguard the girls, their senses on heightened alert. Small sounds coming from unusual places had everyone locked in the house. The girls had gone to their room and were thankfully not underfoot as they usually were.

Jace thought that was enough of an alarm. Those two girls always gave him the creeps. They were just weird most of the time. They were nice, they had never harmed anyone or anything that he knew of, but for some reason, instinct maybe, he was just wary around them.

They were MaMere's grandchildren and he would never say anything about his feelings out of respect, but it didn't change things. In fact, talking with his brothers, he found that most people had the same reservations. It was a feeling of impending doom. Kind of like having a pet tiger cub... you loved it and it was cute, cuddly and playful as a baby, but you knew that it would grow into an enormous adult animal with teeth and claws that would flay you open at the moment you least expected it. Lately, he had noticed that they weren't cubs anymore.

With everything that was going on, every warrior was sent to battle with Ma...er ... Tethys. He was pissed at first, when he was told that he would have to stay behind and babysit, but then Tethys came to him and told him that it was a great honor to be chosen worthy to protect them. It had been explained to him over and over, when he was a child, who and what they were.

The fact that they had aged so slowly over the years, even when most supernatural creatures normally aged slowly, allowed them to go from one stage to another, depending on when they wanted to age themselves. The way they looked into you was the worst. You could feel it, almost as if they were tasting you. He shivered at the thought, again thankful that they had chosen to go to their room and leave Cecile and him to perform guard duty.

His and Cecile's supersensitive hearing was picking up sounds, normal sounds, but not from where they should be coming. His primary bird form was a hawk, so his sight and hearing was his advantage, while Cecile was a Were Cat. Her strength was sight and smell. She was getting the same odd signals.

Armed to the teeth, they both heard a bang and a thumping noise coming from the front room. They both moved forward so fast they were merely a blur, not as much as making a single floorboard creak, or even a scuff from their shoes. Entering the room, they scanned the door, the windows, the ceiling, and turning in a slow circle to back each other when a movement high and to their right had them both drawing down….on Scratchy Patchy.

Shit! The damned little cat almost got shot. She just sat there on the bookshelf blinking at them with her weird little mismatched eyes.

The cat looked at them and then let out a huge mournful, Meeeeeooooorroowooooowww! Meerrorooowwwwww. She began to pace on her perch and suddenly the whole house felt like it bounced on its foundations. The windows and doors blew open, spewing glass and splintered wood everywhere.

They both whirled at the explosion and hit the floor. Smoke filled the room and all was quiet again. Quickly finding their feet, Jace and Cecile moved for cover. Jace tried to upend the massive round table in the dining room and found that even with his superior strength, it wouldn't budge. Instead he grabbed one of the massive shelves that lined the room and flung it to the floor as a shield.

Cecile, armed with a Gladius, had begun her warrior change and motioned to him that she was headed to the back of the house to guard the rear. Keeping the girls between them, they should be able to defend themselves…if the magical wards held.

Mere seconds had passed when figures began to present themselves at the openings. Vampires! They were being over-run with vampires! Pupae staged, they were literally being flung at the house as battering rams. They were piling up bodies and trying to shove them through the openings in an attempt to breach the wards that Tethys had put up to protect the house.

The smoke finally clearing, Jace realized that something had just bombed the house. Only the weakest points had given way in the explosion. The damned cat was still screaming her little head off; every tuft of hair she had left was standing straight up. Back arched, pacing sideways and shredding the shelf, she was using as her perch with her now elongated claws and fangs, her version of warrior form. You had to hand it to the little cat, she was ready to fight!

Jace jumped into action. He began shoving the carcasses back through to keep the wards intact. From the sounds coming from the back of the house, Cecile was doing the same. He took just a moment to run to the girl's room to check on them and make sure they were ready to make an escape, should they be overcome.

He flung the door open to find them calmly standing side by side in their room. They both looked at him as if nothing was wrong. The windows had also been blown out in the room and he saw that the vampires were being hurled at them in here too, only they were hitting some kind of extra shield. Nothing could get within ten feet of the house on this side.

He yelled at them to stay where they were and be ready to run to the escape tunnel if it turned ugly. They just continued to stare without saying another word. Loud bangs and louder screeching brought his attention back to the front of the house. He ran to continue fighting them back.

Getting back to the front, the bodies were piling up faster than he could shove them back out. He used the bookshelf he had flung earlier and put it in place of the now ruined doorway. With the strength and magic of the wards, the shelf somehow secured itself into the opening, sealing it.

Seeing his success, he began to grab other shelves to place before the windows. Fortunately, the damned house was filled with bookshelves. Just as he was getting the last two windows sealed the house jumped again and the doorway blasted open again.

This time the vampires that were coming through weren't fledglings, they were cognizant, mature vamps. Determined and intelligent, they began sacrificing themselves to try to claw through the wards. It only took a few minutes even with Jace working at supernatural speed for them to finally break through. Vampires had invaded MaMere's fortress and the wards were down.

Cecile ran to the girls' room and the three of them had vanished down the escape hatch to the underground tunnels running under the house. He had no idea where the tunnels went. Only Tethys and the crazy cat knew.

Jace squared his shoulders and gripped the sword his father had given him on his fourteenth birthday. It was blessed and forged with what he said were the tears of the damned. He had no illusions that he would die here today, but he would not make it easy.

He had to give Cecile and the girls' time to get away. He was sworn to protect and protect he would, with his last drop of blood.

The vampire that walked through the door was tall and thin with long white hair and red eyes. Jace fought the compelling stare that only a very old master vampire could achieve. He blanked his mind and focused his inner thoughts only on the task at hand.

The thing walked calmly into the room and stood completely still. Jace fought for control, only hearing the lessons of his father over and over in his head. The vampire smiled. Exuding cruelty and malevolence he spoke, "Young hawkling, you are skilled and trained in both mind and body, you have had an excellent teacher, but surely you must know this is the end."

Jace took up a fighting stance and raised his sword. The vampire took a step forward and a small ball of orange, black and white fur launched itself at the vampire's head. Claws slashing his head and eyes, she was like lethal Velcro, the way she stuck to him. He tried to fling her off but as soon as he batted one set of claws away, she struck with another and then with her teeth. It was just the advantage Jace needed and he began to attack as well.

Jace went on the offensive hoping the vampire was distracted with the cat. He lunged, striking for the vampire's gut, only to find him not there. Confused, Jace strengthened his resolve and focused deep within. Listening for telltale movement and displacement of air, Jace struck again whirling and turning to a point directly behind him, he hit his target. He had sliced open the vampire's arm, nearly severing it.

The vampire howled in rage and finally flung the cat from his head. A yowling shriek was silenced in a loud thump, before the vampire moved again. Jace refused to be distracted and concentrated on his task. The vampire examined his arm and drew his own weapon. A double-ended Spear of Kira, deadly in the right hands.

The vampire whirled and struck, faster than the eye could see. Jace, anticipating the maneuver, countered, gaining a slice on his right thigh.

Blades flashed as they danced, retreating and advancing, stabbing and slashing. Jace had gotten lucky with bringing first blood, now it was going to be a test of his skill and training just to survive.

Conserving his strength, Jace's movements were economical and efficient. He blocked each of the vampire's attacks, constantly feeling the mental barrage of manipulation the vampire was sending out. Jace continued to hear his father's voice, *"Conserve your strength, monitor your body's rhythms, control and use the energies around you. Survival means patience and skill... Don't rush, seal your emotions, let your body react with the repetition of its' training."*

Jace moved, twisting to avoid a stab to his heart and ducking for the return stroke, striking low as he moved. Rewarded with a slash to the Achilles tendon, the vampire didn't even flinch, though his wounds were gaping, not healing, due to the oiled salt on Jace's sword. His arm basically useless from Jace's first strike, he attacked unhindered by the need to breath; he continued the dance of death with relish.

Taunting Jace constantly, he conversed as if he were sitting calmly with a cup of tea, "You know this could all be avoided if you would simply surrender and we could have a nice little gentlemanly chat. I have a few questions I would like answered." Duck, jab, slice. "Although I will eventually find what it is I seek, it would save me a considerable amount of time." Whirl, roll, spin, thrust.

Jace didn't listen, he pulled on his reserves, countering every move, seeing the movement a split second ahead as his father had trained him. Jumping, flipping, kicking, and slashing.

"Truth be told, I am quite enjoying myself. It is not often I am able to get a bit of exercise. Helps loosen stiff muscles, you know. This is a very interesting place; I don't suppose you could tell me where the treasure is kept?" A flip up to the ceiling, rolling then spinning back to the floor, the vampire sliced Jace's neck, arm chest and inner thigh, severing his jugular and carotid arteries, all in the time it took for his feet to land on the floor.

Jace fell to his knees, blood pooled on the floor in front of his bowed head and poured from his leg. Still clutching his sword with one arm, he braced his body with the other.

The vampire stood before him, sheathing his weapon behind his back. "Tch, tch, tch. Look at what you have made me do, young hawkling. Have I struck so deep as to disable your vocal chords? No matter, I can retrieve the information I seek when I relieve you of your soul." He grabbed Jace by the front of his shirt and dragged him to his feet.

Jace, nearly unconscious from loss of blood, gathered his remaining strength and made one final strike, to the vampire's dead heart. The vampire simply looked down. "Look at that, you have ruined my shirt. Well done, you have done your duty to your last breath. I will grant you one moment of peace in that knowledge before I take it away. Hmmm...I wonder, could I possibly turn you? It is a thought. Oh yes, what a sweet little experiment you will make."

He shook Jace hard to make his head loll back on his shoulders. Jace looked at him and asked, "Who are you?" The vampire stopped and smiled, evilly. "Who am I? Ahh Ha ha ha ah! Why, young hawkling! Where are my manners? You must forgive me for not making the proper introductions. Haulfgaard Snorey's son, of noble Viking descent. More in keeping with modern times, I am called Hal Sorenson. I am the first child of The Mariner, Owner of that ship of damnation that returned to its home port, less its cargo and crew. It was I, who boarded my ship in wonder and awe that it had gone missing for five years without a trace. It was my own blood that first slaked the throat of The Mariner. You might say that I am the Prince of Vampires."

Then the vampires jaws elongated, his glamour dropped and his true image emerged. An animated skull, shrouded in petrified muscle and flesh, burning black eyeballs with glowing red pupils and rows and rows of needle sharp teeth, dripping with venom and a black coiling worm of a tongue snaked out and chomped down on what remained of Jace's neck and shoulder.

A maniacal howl erupted from the corner of the room and an elongating tornado of claws and teeth descended once again on the vampires head. Scratchy was growing into a full blown warrior form, attacking for all she was worth. To Jace, she was worth *his* weight in revenge as he closed his eyes for the last time.

Once again the vampire tried to detach himself from those shredding blades that had now grown into six inch claws attached to a fully grown were-tigress calico-kitty-something. Fangs sunk deep into his emaciated bone and flesh. Kicking, tearing and shredding him alive… or actually dead in his case.

She had somehow stolen the vampire's own spear and was using it against him. She had again caught him off-guard and gave such a feverish attack that can only be described as insane. Matching him in strength and speed, she filleted him where he stood. Finally falling to the floor, he moved in jerking motions for a moment and then was still.

Scratchy, or Bernice, now out of her little kitty form, picked Jace up and drug him to the overturned sofa, righted it and lay him down. She ran to the bookshelf that she had been pacing on and grabbed the old wooden cup that was being used as a bookend for the Gutenberg Bible, one of the many rare books in MaMere's collection and ran back to Jace. She bit hard on her own paw and squeezed a few drops of blood into the cup. She swirled it around a moment and said a prayer, then she tilted Jace's head to the side and poured the blood over his wounds and threw the cup down beside her and held and rocked the young man, praying fervently.

Immediately, his wounds began to heal. His body jerked and thrashed. His heart struggled to beat once again. She cradled him in her lap and comforted him while his soul returned to its owner. After a few moments, he was still, asleep in exhaustion.

A small sound behind her made her turn. The vampire was up and he had the cup. He smiled and raised the cup to his lips, laughing in delight. "I knew that one of you would use the cup to save your comrades from a soulless existence or death! You even prayed over it for me, how wonderful, how complete!" The cup poised over his mouth, about to spill the remaining drops of life-giving holy blood into a demon of death. Holding Jace as she was, Bernice could not move fast enough to stop him.

That gaping maw, wide open as the first drop spilled toward his lips, the cup was jerked from his hands and flew into awaiting hands down the hall. In the hallway stood the girls,   They had used their powers to remove his prize.

One single drop of bright red blood hissed and smoked on those evil lips. The black tongue flicked it inside the mouth in less than a blink. In the second blink, the vampire was gone.

25 AN ETERNITY OF IMPRISONMENT

The chained man whispered for Max to be still. Max glared at him thinking that the man was irritated at his efforts to break his bonds. The man, seeing the glare, spoke softly, "Every time you tug on that chain, you feed Mab. Look at where the chain leads."

Max looked, followed the line of the chain where it came out of a wall of rock. It wasn't secured by a bolt, but continued up through a hole in the ceiling of the chamber.

Looking back at the man, he nodded and stopped straining to break them. "Conserve your strength," the man whispered. "You'll need it soon. I know every tunnel, every nook and cranny of this place. I also know the sounds and vibrations that connect the tunnels. There is an army encamped close by, presumably to rescue the two of you. I can also feel a strange movement in one of the unused tunnels. When they come for you, free me and I will guide you out of this place. Don't… and you will be lost in these tunnels forever."

Max nodded and closed his eyes to save his strength and try again to contact Sam. Relieved, he found she was nearby and not in distress. Puzzled, because the last time he was able to reach her, she was in the middle of the biggest and most terrifying time of her life. Now, all of a sudden, she was fine? She had him worried out of his mind. Had Tethys done something to affect her fertility cycles? He pushed again, bombarding her with questions.

Sam responded dreamily that she was close and they were working on a way to get him out of there. Max griped that she sounded fine now, was she just going through another female thing or what? Instead of blasting back at him, she simply said, "You could say that I have found my mate."

Max jumped, gaining another glare from the chained man, "There's another male dragon! Where did he come from? It has to be a trick, there are no dragons left of our kind!"

She sighed and said, "You aren't the only one who can learn to adapt for love, dear brother. I never said he was a dragon. Actually, he is an elf."

"An elf! You've got to be kidding me! You still can't mate! Love and mushy stuff is one thing, but biology is another! When your eggs begin to gestate, you will have to get them fertilized, they will rot and poison your body and it will kill you! Those are the simple facts...dear sister!"

"Go choke on smoke, Max! The point is he makes me feel better. I was stuck in a half form and bleeding. Since I met him, I have been able to fully change and the bleeding and pain has stopped. He is definitely having some kind of effect on my *biology*. I don't know if I can actually mate with him, yet I haven't had a chance to ask him." Max huffed, "Just how long have you known this guy?" Sam hesitated and said, "Not too long, we just met a few minutes ago." Max roared in his frustration and heard the goblin come running to investigate, gaining another glare from the chained man."

The goblin walked over to Max and inspected the chain that bound him. He must have loosened it a little with his thrashing, because the goblin adjusted the slack and kicked Max in the ribs for disturbing his nap as he stomped back to wherever he came from.

A pained moan came from the floor where Justin lay. Max must have roused him into consciousness with all the noise he was making. The chained man spoke again to Justin, "Don't move against your bonds, Mab feeds on pain. The more you move the more pain you will be in. Breath in deeply and release your breath slowly, exhaling the pain with it."

Max realized the man was trying to help. "Who are you?" The man was stunned. It had been a very long time since he had thought about who he was. "My name is Troy Endres. I believe I know all about you, based on your discussion with Mab earlier. Tell me please, what year is it?"

Max had never contemplated those facts. As a dragon, the recording of time was irrelevant. Only the changes in the man's development made any impact. He didn't answer.

Justin blew out painfully, "It is the year two thousand and twelve." Troy simply closed his eyes and leaned his head back against the rock wall behind him. Max asked him, "What manner of beast are you that Mab captured you?" The man was quiet, in thought, and finally he replied, "I am just an ordinary man, I think. I really don't know why she captured me. I was just a farmer's son. One day I was working in my father's fields in Greenland and a group of men came marching down the road. They saw me working and grabbed me and tied me up and dumped me in the back of a wagon. From there I was dumped on a ship bound for the West Indies and was pressed into service on a merchant ship as a deckhand. I was twelve at the time.

When I was fourteen, I was allowed to go ashore with the rest of the crew when we were in port. One night we were in a tavern drinking in Spain and I got clubbed over the head. When I woke, I was here...chained as you see me now. Mab releases me to repair her tunnels. When the repairs are finished, she returns me to my chains. I have often wondered, why me? There is nothing special about me. Yes, I have grown tall and strong, that is obvious for anyone to see, but that is the result of many hours of hard labor. I am not immortal that I am aware. I do know that I was born in the year 1607. Something is keeping me alive all these years, though I have often prayed for death. I exist and continue to exist, that is all I know."

Hearing Troy's story, Justin closed his eyes and continued to breathe deeply; conserving his strength for what he prayed was a speedy rescue. He refused to accept that he could be kept Mab's prisoner for hundreds of years...or more.

Max also heard the man's story. As a dragon, he had taken naps longer than that, but never as a prisoner, never in pain and never with the very real threat of having his bones sucked dry. He too prayed for a speedy rescue.

The three men were silent with their own thoughts, trying to deal with the pain of their imprisonment, for some time when they heard splashing noises. Looking all around, it seemed the noises were coming from the little water well that was situated to one side of the chamber.

All three men were instantly alert, listening, hoping the end was near. Max finally whispered, "Who's there?" A little more scrabbling and splashing and a familiar voice rang out, "It's me Lizard Boy! *Somebody* had to come drag your scaly butt out of here."

Max's heart nearly exploded in his chest. "Splash? How did you get here! Please be careful! If Mab discovers you, she will kill you!" Troy hissed at Max, "Be still! If you start thrashing too hard, you will get her attention again!" Splash heard a new voice, "Who's up there with you?"

"He's a friend. Be very quiet, there are guards everywhere." They heard struggling noises and scratching on the walls of the well. "What are you doing? I told you to be quiet!"

"Go suck on sludge, Lizard Boy! I am *trying* to get to this metal grate blocking my way. There is an opening in the middle of the grate, but it's too small for me to get through and it's too high up for me to reach with one claw. I need a rope or something."

Troy spoke up, "I have an idea. Max, can you make your skin look a little more damaged or something?" Max was a little confused where this was going, so he complied and tried to change again and it resulted in scale-like impressions on his skin, so he held that position and said, "How's this?"

"Good, real good, now shut your eyes and act like you are dying and don't move and tell your friend in the well not to make a single sound and be ready to grab the rope." Troy waited a moment for everyone to get still and quiet. He took a deep breath and yelled,

"Gaarrrkkk! You pile of worm-shit, you have let Mab's prisoner die! She will flay the skin of your testicles for the next thousand years for this! HA HA!" He took another breath and calculated the time it would take for the goblin to come running to check it out.

He yelled again, "I can't wait to be the one to break the news! He started out less loudly, Maaaaabbb! Your draaagoooon is deeaaadd!" Then a little louder, "Hey Maaaabbbb, Gark let your dragon die of thiiiirssstt!" He began again, "Heeyy Maaa" SMACK, the goblin, Gark, punched Troy in the mouth and said, "Say another word, digger man, and I will cut out your tongue."

The goblin ran to the well and dropped down a bucket on a rope into the well. The bucket fell down and splashed into the water for a second and Splash just missed it by a hair when the Goblin snatched it back up again. He ran back and threw the water in Max's face. Max cracked his eyes open a slit and Troy vigorously shook his head no, so Max didn't move a muscle. Gark waited a moment, watching, and when nothing happened he kicked at the chains, but Max remained motionless.

Convinced that something was wrong with the prisoner, he ran back to the well for more water. Down went the bucket into the well. This time Splash was ready and she grabbed hold of the bucket and wound the rope around her arm and yanked hard. The goblin reacted out of instinct and pulled up just as hard. Goblins were known for being brutes; the force that was exerted on the grate with Splash braced and pushing in the same direction had the effect of a projectile coming up out of the well. Splash and the grate were propelled right on up and out of the well to land on top of the goblin.

Splash was fast and she grabbed the grate and bashed the goblin in the head, knocking him out. For good measure she hit him a couple more times with the bucket.

Splash stood on still shaky legs and wobbled over to where Max lay chained. She reached out to touch the chain and Troy screamed out, "No! Don't touch the chain! Mab will feel it. Release me and I will show you how to free him." Splash turned and said, "Yeah right, I release you and you take off, leaving me here to get caught. No thanks pal."

She reached for him again and Troy yelled, "Max, stop her! She will accomplish nothing but getting herself killed and alerting Mab that there is a rescue party trying to free you. You will not only get her killed but she will reinforce those chains and you won't have a prayer in the wind of ever being free! You have to trust me!"

Max nodded and Splash dropped her hands. "Splash, please... go free him first, he's right. I can feel the connection through the chains draining me. Mab will know the moment you touch them." She scrambled back upright and loped over to where Troy was chained.

Troy breathed a sigh of relief and said, "All these chains and restraints are rigged. You have to know exactly how to release them or you will trigger poison gases imbedded in the walls. They all looked around to see the little holes that dotted the walls and ceilings.

Splash smirked and turned back to him, "Why didn't you tell me that to start with?" Troy returned her smirk and said, "Would it have made a difference?" Splash shrugged, "Probably not. Ok, let's do this thang."

Troy told her that the lock on the chains was only a decoy and another trigger. The latch was actually secured through the metal loop above his head. The trick was to release both latches at the same time, hold them down and release the chains. If one latch was open only slightly more than the other, it would trigger the gas.

That wasn't the biggest problem. Though Splash was a big creature for a female, she was still only barely over six feet. She couldn't jump or stretch for it. She would need a ladder to reach the latch. Troy, seeing the problem, slid down as far as he could, tightening the chains that were around his neck and bent his legs so she could stand on his knees.

Sounds simple, right? Oh, but let's not forget that Splash is just learning to use her legs. Wobbling all over the place, she stepped up on his knees. Leaning against the wall to brace herself with one hand, she examined the latches. She was going to need both hands to do this. She leaned her entire body into Troy's frame for balance.

Since his hands were chained, he couldn't hold on to her to steady her. So he leaned his head to one side as much as he could with the chains tightened on his neck, to give her something more to brace herself.

Suddenly they heard someone come trudging down the tunnel. Everyone held their breath. A loud grunt. A second guard had discovered the one Splash knocked out.

The guard started slapping the one knocked out to revive him, yelling something about being drunk. Troy saw that as soon as Gaark woke, they would sound the alarm-they were going to be caught. They were so close!   Seeing his chances of freedom being snatched away, Troy reacted instinctively and roared, standing up to his full height, dumping Splash on the floor just as she had disabled the trigger and surged forward on his chains. The sudden heaving on rusted bolts and links was more than they could take. Bolts and chains snapped, some of the stones holding the bindings were pulled loose and disintegrated.

Not losing any forward momentum, Troy ran to the guards, meeting them head on. He slammed his huge fist in the already injured Gark's face, dropping him like a rock once again. He whirled and grabbed the other guard's head in his massive arms and squeezed and twisted, snapping his neck. He dropped the dead goblin and Splash found her footing and made sure the other would never wake again.

They both stood, breathing hard, staring at each other. Splash huffed, "Why didn't you do that to begin with?" Troy, looking a little surprised, "I didn't know I could." Splash looked at him sarcastically, "Dude, have you looked in a mirror lately?"

Justin moaned and tried to continue to remain still. They both turned and went over to where Max and Justin lay. Troy reached out to disentangle their chains and realized he needed to get rid of his chains first so as not to trigger any more alarms than necessary. He began pulling on the chains attached to the shackle around his neck. He couldn't pull hard enough without strangling himself.

Splash, seeing the problem said, "Here, sit on the floor. I am going to pull on the shackle one way; you pull on the chain the other. She wrapped her hands around the shackle and braced her legs on his thigh. He grabbed the other chain with both hands. Splash said, "Ok, on the count of three pull for your life. One, Two, Three!" Splash heaved backwards, stiffening her legs into iron girders. Troy, remembering her words, pulled for his life. Screeeeechh, Ping! It worked!

From there it was a simple matter of unthreading the chains from his hands and feet, as they had been connected to his neck shackle. Releasing the actual shackles could wait till later. Once free, Troy rushed to Justin and picked up a rock and started grinding the rope away. Seeing Splash's puzzled look, he explained, "Mab will know the second you touch the rope. We have to free this guy first so he can help us with Lizard Boy. They have been touching each other the whole time, so she won't notice the strange presence when he grabs the chain." Splash picked up another rock and began sawing on the ropes as well.

It seemed like an eternity, but in fact it was only about two minutes and they had severed the ropes from Justin. Justin continued to moan and lay there. Troy looked at him and told Splash, "Go get water. It must be the wolfsbane; we need to wash it off him."

She ran back to the well and filled the bucket four times before Justin began to revive. As soon as he did, he began to change into his warrior form. Faster than the movies, but they got it right with the sounds of bones crunching, growing and changing. Justin, finishing his change, stood as tall as Troy. Maybe a little taller, it was hard to tell.

Bending over, Troy explained how Max's restraints worked. It was basically a slip knot with a control strand of bones in the middle. The prey was snatched up from underneath, encircling them. A large bone with a hole bored from its center was used to gather the loose ends tight. To free Max, Justin would have to slide the bone up and relieve the tension on the net. They still couldn't touch the net or Max, so Max would have to use what strength he had left to wiggle slowly by himself. Troy also explained that the bones were connected by a loop around Mab's waist so that she could feed from and monitor her captive. He told them of his plan.

26 A NEW BALANCE OF POWER

The girls held the cup, now only stained by the blood it just contained and carefully put it back on the shelf, next to the Bible it braced only moments before. They walked over to Bernice, still in her ferocious calico tiger cat form. She looked up at them, apologizing for her failure to stop the vampire.

"Shhh….rest and heal your wounds,

you have not failed," Adey said in her weird 'balance voice' as she stroked Bernice's fur. "You have saved another soldier of God to fight again. You could not have foreseen the vampire's trickery, for it was unplanned and instinctive in his evil nature – inevitable, really. He has been searching for a way to gain access to the cup for centuries. It was only a matter of time before he would find his opportunity."

A bang from the back rooms and Cecile came running down the hallway to find them. "How did you get away from me? We have to go! The vampires will kill you!" She blinked, looking around and seeing the carnage that had taken place in the front of the house. Shelves were pulled down, books scattered everywhere and Jace, still bloody and lying in Bernice's lap, both unconscious. Cecile ran over to them and checked their pulse and found they were both still very much alive.

Cecile dug her cell phone out of her pocket again and cursed, "Damn! Still no signal! We have to get help. We have to let someone know what has happened here. Come on, let's go!"

Maddey walked over to Cecile and took her hand and led her to a chair, gently pushing her to sit down. You could see that she was struggling to argue her point, but suddenly she didn't know what the point could possibly be.

Maddey leaned over and whispered in her ear, "Listen carefully, I have a message I want you to give to Tethys when she finds you. You have to make sure and get it exactly right, do you understand, Cecile?"

Cecile looked back at Maddey with round blank eyes and nodded dumbly. Maddey leaned closer and whispered the message in her ear. "You must stay awake and alert to protect the others. Do not let anyone else in the house that doesn't belong here, ok?" Again Cecile nodded and sat in her chair to wait.

Jace still unconscious, Cecile taken care of and Bernice in a blissful, healing sleep, the girls walked outside the house to the yard. Vampires still milling about noticed new prey and ran to attack, only to be thrown back, smoking and boiling from the inside out by a mysterious force surrounding the now glowing young women. All those in the vicinity dropped to the ground to die. Those that remained fled for survival.

Facing each other, the girls embraced, hugging each other.

Immense power filled the air to the point of becoming a suffocating vacuum, the pressure was intense. A small tornado began to form all around them, lifting them into the air and whisking them away into the clouds.

27 WHY DIDN'T YOU DO THAT BEFORE?

Everyone was ready to move. Justin had slid the bone up to relieve the tension in the net. Max struggled and panted, using every bit of strength he had to wiggle free of the net. He had to do it slowly so Mab wouldn't get suspicious. It was pure agony for him.

Finally free, Troy instructed him to

continue to hold onto the net so as not to break the connection. Troy told Justin to climb the chain to the ceiling and be ready to jamb a vicious looking metal torture spike into the chain to keep it from being pulled through on the other side.

Troy and Splash were in place while Max carefully gathered the net in his hands. Troy said, "Ok, just like before, on three and we all pull like hell. Ready...One, two, three!" Max pulled down hard and Troy and Splash grabbed him around the waist and pulled too. The three of them turned and ran until all the slack from the chains was pulled taut. At that moment, Justin slammed the makeshift cotter-pin into the chain and they took off running down the tunnels.   As they ran, they could hear horrible bellows and inhuman screeching from above.

Mab was pacing her chambers. She knew that Tethys was encamped less than a mile away. At the present moment, she was having two of Tethys's loyal gnomes, dismembered a little at a time, trying to get strategic information out of them. Neither of them was giving her anything useful.

She was frustrated beyond reason.

How could creatures of her own kingdom commit such treachery to her enemies? Was she not their queen and bound to serve her? Past the point of getting any information other than the state of their pathetic lives and how *good it was* working for Tethys, she allowed them no respite from the slow torture of pulling each little appendage and protrusion from their bodies.

Tethys had formed a barrier around the camp. She couldn't even get one spy in to reconnoiter specifics about strength, numbers or battle plans. She paced, she cursed, she hurt things-but she was elated. All of her careful planning was coming to fruition.

If not for waiting for the damned vampire, she would have already launched her own attack. She was waiting for him to bring the added troops, for the terror they would create, and to add to the numbers of her own army. Where in the hell was he?

Flopping down on her divan, she flung her hand to her head to think how to make him pay for making her wait like this. About to give an order to have someone go search for him she was suddenly yanked off her couch and dragged to the hole in the floor by her dragon bone chain.

She couldn't get loose! She screamed and struggled, but she couldn't break the chain. That was the point of the chain, wasn't it? It couldn't be broken by anything but another dragon! She was trapped. She screamed and ordered the guards to the chamber below to release the chain. Her captives were getting away!

Troy, Splash, Max and Justin ran for their lives. Troy was in the lead and Splash thanked God that she had relented and given in to his demands to be released first, so that he was now with them guiding them around these demented hellholes. The maze of tunnels were so confusing that several times they could have sworn they were in the same tunnel only to be proven wrong.

The traps were deadly. What looked like a puddle was a deep pool of flesh dissolving acid, stepping on the wrong rock would create a cave-in, poison gases or spikes, or you could stumble into a cave with a very hungry, very large beast in it. Some even contained spells that would make you forget…everything, including how to breathe.

Splash argued that they didn't have to be stealthy because Mab already knew they were free, so why be quiet? Troy said sarcastically, "fine, make all the noise you want and let her know exactly where to find you!" "Oh, when you put it that way..." She whispered from then on out.

They had turned into what Troy said was the last tunnel and found themselves faced with a giant, pinkish white slug? When it opened its hole of a mouth, and they found out how Mab had been able to dig tunnels so fast.

"It's a Wyrm" Troy whispered, signaling them to halt. "It has fifty rotating rows of giant serrated teeth that bore into the earth, eating and chewing its way down into the core, all controlled by scent. They have no eyes and only the scent glands guide them to food. They love the scent of rotted meat." Although, as Troy explained further, they would eat anything that got in their way or anything that threatened them.

Splash asked Troy, "Um... excuse me, but shouldn't we be going the other way?" Troy said, "They are incredibly fast, we would never make it. This one isn't acting like it's threatened, but if we run it will think of food and chase us down. Our best bet is to stand still, stay out of the way of the mouth and hope it goes on past us."

Noises were coming from the other end of the tunnel and the Wyrm was on the attack. Splash turned to Troy, "What do we do now?" Troy said, "I don't know, either way we go, we will be killed."

Max, now really amused said, "Uh, guys… I feel fine now, I can get us out." Troy looked at Max and said, "Take it easy, little guy, this is no time to be a hero and no time for jokes." Max, now highly offended, didn't say anything, just started changing. First, his human eyes were nice and blue, then they turned a nice reptile green and the pupil got larger and erupted into a split and grew and grew. Then there were teeth, lots and lots of really long, really sharp teeth.

Troy mimicked Splash's earlier comment, "Why didn't you do that before?" Then Max blew a heated snort at Troy, giving him a slight steam burn. He stepped around Troy, opened his mouth and blew flame into the Wyrm until it was completely incinerated.

It took a moment before the other three were ready to move again, the fire having sucked up all the available oxygen in that part of the tunnel. They started running and then at an appropriate spot, Max stopped and blew more flame at another spot and began to dig wildly until light from above peaked down at them. Max hoisted them all up through the hole and then he turned and blasted super-heated flames back down the tunnel into Mab's guards and then he jumped through the hole himself.

Tethys and the others were working out different strategies when Sam jumped; she had been glued to Bataar's side since he had held her. She hadn't spoken a word, but she never let him move more than three feet from her. She shouted, "He's free! Splash has released him from the chains and they are on their way! He needs passage through the barrier Tethys set up...and uh...he wants me to tell you that there are four of them?"

28 WYRMS!

The same moment Tethys dropped her wards, the ground buckled up beneath their feet. Everyone was thrown off balance as if a bomb had gone off underground. Tethys quickly raised the wards again, making a mental connection with Splash the second they were safe.

The next second giant slugs were

bursting through the earth everywhere.
"Wyrms!" Bataar and Tethys shouted.
Bataar shouted, "No one move! They
sense the vibrations of movement and
are too fast to outrun!" Tethys
conveyed his instructions telepathically
to her troops. Everyone froze in place.
Tethys murmured, "I wondered how she
was able to move her sidhes around so
quickly," and kicked herself mentally for
her oversight. Bataar gave her a
pointed look and said, "You have much
to learn about the resources available to
one such as Mab, my friend."

A second round of rumbling from
under the earth and Max came bursting
through, spewing white hot flame. Sam
jumped in the air and followed suit. Any
creatures capable of flight also took to
the air spewing flame, poisons, arrows
and any matter of destructive forces of
which they were capable.

Though they fought valiantly, there
were many more Wyrms than anyone
thought possible. Like a bubbling pile of
maggots, they just kept coming. It was
impossible to avoid them and many of
Tethys's forces were gobbled up in
attempts to flee or fight.

Hawk, Tethys, Dan and Jamie used
their telepathic abilities to organize

everyone. They rallied the troops into defense positions. Coordinated attacks from above and below were quickly put into place. Supernatural creatures with a talent for speed were used as bait and diversions to maximize air bombing raids from above.

Slowly, they began to see an end to the frenzy of the surprise attack. The remaining Wyrms were dispatched on the ground and surrounding them in an all-out assault. Blades singing, teeth and claws flashing, many of the remaining Wyrms were converted to masses of shredded tissue and meat. Tissue that was quickly consumed and converted to fuel by the dragons and wyverns, Weres and any other creatures that needed recharging. Unfortunately, it also created a bloodlust that was quickly rising in the ranks of Tethys soldiers.

Fearful that having so many different factions of enemies united under a tenuous truce might forget their promises of loyalty for a common cause, Tethys concentrated hard at sending out waves of thought, focusing her energies on the real enemies at hand.

Just when they were about to taste their first real victory, the ground began to rumble and shake a third time. This time the entire area began to collapse beneath them. Mab had been more than prepared than Tethys had given her credit for, literally falling right into her clutches. She had grievously underestimated her enemy's abilities.

In the time that Tethys had been encamped within her wards of protection, Mab had kept the wryms busy, digging deep underneath them creating tunnels that would turn into trenches in the collapse. They designed to divide and weaken Tethys troops. The very tunnels that Max, Troy, Justin and Splash had risked everything to escape from were once again going to put all their lives in peril. Yes, Mab was a cunning strategist and an expert in underground warfare.

Many were killed in the cave-ins that were happening all around them. Cut off and disconcerted, Tethys troops again began to flounder.

The air support of Hawk, Sam and Max proved invaluable at giving them a new sense of direction and focus, while Troy stepped up and gave them insight at what traps would be lying in wait for them. He quickly told Tethys what signs to look for when navigating the new tunnels-turned-trenches of death.

Tethys began to weaken being suddenly separated from the nutrients of water and the excursion of being a mental communications center, though she had dropped her now useless wards, her first wall of defense.

She turned to Hawk to direct her from above to the nearest source of water to recharge. Hawk simply swooped down and grabbed her up in his great talons and gave her a good dunking in the stream they had previously used as a feeder route to get to this location.

Though she had underestimated the direction of Mab's initial method of attack, she, too, had a few tricks up her sleeve.

29 SO YOU WANT TO FIGHT DIRTY

Freshly recharged and ready to fight, Tethys directed Hawk to her secondary position. Instructing her troops to initiate phase two, she took stock of her troops and weapons.

Instead of navigating the trenches as Mab expected and bringing the battle to certain defeat within Mab's own lair, Tethys was going to draw her out in the open where she would be much more vulnerable.

Before they ever left the island on Old Lady Lake, with Lucky's help and military expertise, they had quickly taken stock of the size of their allies' strengths and instructed them to send only a small initial contingent as a distraction while they made a big show of converging on a field of battle close to Mab's lair.   Tethys instructed everyone to climb to the top of the trench they were in and await air transport via the flying creatures and the floats they rode in on to the fallback position and the real battlefield. A battlefield that had been prepped with fortifications and included a lake freshly infused with salt water, a battleground more suited to her troops' inherent talents and a whole new army of reinforcements.

Due to modern technology, innovation and a virtually limitless source of funds, Tethys had arranged to have her new battlefield reinforced with iron. While they had been busy creating the distraction of the first encampment, Lucky had arranged a construction crew to pound into the ground a moat closely spaced of iron rebar inserted into tubes also made from iron, shipped overnight from a steel mill nearby. Iron is lethal to most varieties of Fae. The bars didn't have to be strong, they just had to be iron.

Several human construction crews were paid handsomely to work through the night to complete the task, hence the reason Tethys stalled for time, "waiting for Hawk to arrive." The scent and activity of humans with large machinery was such a common site, Mab never questioned what they were working on. Tethys had not been the only one to underestimate the depths of her enemies' resources.

The iron tubes contained charges in the bottom so that when triggered, they would propel the graduated rods of rebar inside up above the ground through chains of graduating sizes creating an instant fence or cage twenty feet high and twenty feet deep, impossible for any Fae to scale above or below, unless you had the ability of flight. Just as a precaution, nets were on hand for that possibility as well.

Several lines of reinforcements awaited her command. No matter what Mab threw at her she would eventually run out of resources. Tethys' plan was not to run in with everything she had - guns blazing, so to speak, but to taunt Mab with a seemingly small army with weak defenses.

Tethys surmised that Mab had been waiting a long time for this chance to extract her vengeance and she would be impatient to see it come to fruition. She hoped that Mab would throw caution to the wind and hit them with her best weapons first. Although Wyrms had not occurred to Tethys, the strength of the attack was not entirely unexpected and spoke volumes of what Mab's strength really was.

Sam and Max were an unexpected surprise in dealing with the Wyrms and they dispatched them more quickly than Tethys anticipated with their fiery breaths. Because of their strength, she didn't need to employ a valuable resource that she could now use later on.

If the Wyrms were Mab's best, then she had already beaten that. The only thing stronger would be Mab herself. Feeling the battle spirit beating strong in her heart to defend her family, friends and territory, Tethys virtually shivered in anticipation.

Yes, it *had* been a long time since

she was engaged in a battle with such a worthy adversary, using all her skills as honed warrior and leader; she anxiously awaited Mab's second attack.

All the troops had regrouped and were now even more confident in Tethys leadership. There were some casualties, as was expected when they entered into battle, but the plan worked perfectly. Their resolve that Mab's tyranny would soon come to an end galvanized them into seeing this thing through, once and for all.

Bloodlust still running high in some, the waiting became excruciating, but patience was stressed. They couldn't risk the chance of springing the trap too soon and missing their chance, so those that had the savagery in their eyes were given the work of burying the bodies of the slain or what was left of them.

In the meantime Tethys paced the field, checking and double checking the perimeter. Hawk and his squadron patrolled the skies; the Weres stalked the outlying woods and forest sniffing for any odd scent or sign of attack.

Lucky and Jamie were busy communicating strategy to the ranks. Bataar had grabbed Troy and myself and began training for those inexperienced soldiers in effective combat and fighting techniques. Everyone was trained, including the little gnomes. Sam and Max grumbled, complaining that they were great dragons and had no need of this kind of hand-to-hand training. Bataar simply replied, "Max, how did that work for you when you were trapped as a human in Mab's clutches?" He relented and fell into step as the group completed their exercises.

Seeing a natural warrior in Troy, he asked him if he knew why Mab had taken him prisoner. When Troy told him that he had begged her to tell him why, she had never given him even the most remote clue. That was what had made it so hard for Troy all these years... why him? Troy asked Bataar if he knew and Bataar nodded, but told him that he should seek out Tethys first to remove the mental barriers Mab had placed on him. Then he continued his training instruction.

Troy, eager to finally know the truth, went in search of Tethys. He found her walking the perimeter. She was so concentrated on what she was doing, she barely noticed his approach. "Excuse me Tethys, Ma'am, we haven't been introduced, my name is Troy

Endres. I escaped Mab's tunnels with Max. Bataar told me to ask you if you could help me with something." Tethys was irritated at having her thoughts interrupted and was about to brush him off when she glanced in his direction. She looked at him a second time, more closely and said, "You look familiar to me. What is your name again?" Encouraged, Troy repeated his name and his request. Tethys put her hands on either side of his face and looked deep into his eyes.

"Yesss, I know you...Godling."
"Huh?" Troy was confused. "What do you mean?" Tethys smiled and sniffed in his aroma, breathing deep. "I thought there were no more like you in existence. I recognize the scent of power in your blood. I called you a Godling; a descendent of a God, the mighty Thor was the father of your kin. You are not a god, but you carry the strength, the long life and strangely, much power. Do you not know your parentage?"

Now very confused and just a little offended, Troy responded, "My parents were farmers and I was taken from them when I was a young boy."

Tethys continued to smile, "Bataar is

wise. I will help you see your past to clear your head. Mab was shrewd to get you before your power was fully mature. She fed on your strength, could you not feel it?" Troy began to close his eyes as Tethys began to unravel the cobwebs of confusion blocking his memories.

She saw the torture Mab had put the poor man through. She saw him drained cruelly to the point of death many times, because he didn't know how to protect himself from her cruel magic. She saw his agony, being kept like an animal for so many years.

She cleared those cobwebs and mists of evil magic from his mind, healed the wounds that had scarred him so cruelly and showed him the legend of his ancestry. She showed him how to contain his strength to make him invulnerable to Mab and any others that would wish him harm.

Then, she showed him her own experience with the Lord, God. She showed him how magic had been pulled from the Earth to create the gods of Vikings, Greeks, Romans and many others by man's impatience during the Lord's time of rest. She showed him that without him there is no real hope. She showed him that all magic comes from He who made the Earth. She showed him that faith in Him makes anything possible. She showed him the history of mankind. She revealed to him who he really was.

When she removed her hands, tears streamed down Troy's cheeks. So grateful for her help, there were no words to express his feelings. He began to go down on bended knee and she stopped him and explained.

"Troy, yes, I am a goddess that was created by man's prayers for magic in times of hardship and ignorance. There is much magic in this world, as the Lord created a wonderful Earth, full of magic. When the Lord wakened after his long slumber, he cast out all other gods. I was spared so that I could serve Him now and forever, the true source of all power. Do not bow to me, for I am merely His servant. I continue to exist to serve Him and carry out His message. I am His soldier. I protect mankind in all their different forms. Human kind thinks it is unique in His Love; He has created us all. So I protect all that serve Him."

She continued with advice and a warning, "Troy, go find your weapon that communes with your heart, but beware, you are mortal, you can die and you can be hurt. You are much stronger and will heal more quickly. You will also live much longer as a testament to your ancestry, but know that you are still human in every other way. You have had much of your long life taken away from you by Mab. Now that you are master of your life, do not waste another minute. Learn to live, love and laugh till the very end." Troy nodded, squeezed her hands in his and walked away, thinking hard about what she said to him.

Tethys watched him go. She turned and used her powers to send a powerful summons to Mab, "Mab, evil Queen of Fairie, your days of cruelty on this earth have come to an end! You will no longer torment your own race or others one minute longer! I command you to meet me now, bitch, for I have come to spill your blood!" Tethys slammed her staff onto the ground sending out a rippling thunder that split the ground all the way to the center of the Sidhe. "And don't keep me waiting!"

30 THE BITCH BITES

Finally released from the chain of dragon's bones, Mab collapsed face down on the rugs and pelts that she had collected and thrown about the floor of her chamber. She lay prone, panting in her rage, shaking with fury at the news of the escape of her captives and howling like an animal at the loss of her most precious Wyrms.

The vampire entered her chamber and stood awaiting her recognition. She raised herself up to float above the floor, her magic buffeting her body like an evil storm.

Calmly she addressed him, "Vampire, you have decided to present yourself in my chamber?" Hal Sorenson smirked and raised an eyebrow, "Has the queen been troubled whilst I did her bidding?"

Mab narrowed her eyes at the audacity of his cleverness. Seething with anger, she hissed, "Hal Sorenson, pray tell us what services you have performed on our behalf!"

Hal strode forward, examined her divan and deposited himself on it with a flourish of grace only a vampire could manage. He lay with his wrist upon his brow, "My dear Queen Mab, for I have given my life as I knew it in your service!" He turned his head to gaze into her eyes, "For you may test the truth of my words."

Once again, faster than an eye could track, the cup was presented to him for the test. In a flash he was standing before her holding the cup in his own hands. Never looking away from her gaze, he spat blood into the cup.

Moving just as quickly as he, Mab

had taken the cup and moved about the room, collecting the ingredients to complete the test. Locking eyes with him, she spat her own into the cup, the catalyst of the truth spell.

She watched the cup like a predator about to strike. Nothing, not even a wisp of smoke, appeared. She quickly raised her eyes to his again, now glowing in her fervor. "The vampire speaks words of truth." She sneered and appeared in a flash directly before him, virtually touching noses, "What have you gained for such a precious price, Mr. Sorenson?"

He never blinked, never hesitated; he danced with her step for step in those words of venom. "Queen Mab, I have acquired that which was agreed to in our pact. What progress have you made to honor *your* part of our agreement, Lady Fae?"

Mab smiled, "You have brought me the army of mature vampires to command?" Hal tilted his chin and motioned with his hand and vampires began pouring into the small chamber. Not the pupae, blood-crazed newborns, but mature, intelligent vampires capable of decimating entire races of beings under the correct direction. Never before had vampires come together in such numbers, other than to kill one another for superiority or territory.

Forgetting her anger, Mab's delight was evident. "What say you, vampires? You will fight under my command without question?" A moment of silence and the vampires gazed upon their real leader for consent. Hal turned back to her, hands behind his back; he inclined his back a mere inch or two and lowered his head, "We await your orders."

Knowing full well that should anything go wrong, the vampires would turn on her. She was prepared for that when she made her request. Mr. Sorenson may be their general, but he would never live to take her down.

Mab began to give orders to her guards when Hal interrupted her. "Forgive me, dear Queen, but you have not answered my question." "What question have you posed?" Hal stood straight and firm, "Have you met the requirements of your part of our agreement?"

Mab had been hoping to use her hostage as a bargaining tool, just in case there was trouble, but now she was forced by the terms of her own agreement to comply. She turned to the guard, "Bring in The Mariner."

Moments later three large goblins came carrying a large tank into the room covered by a large cloth. They set the cylinder upright and pulled the cloth away. The tank was filled with thick red liquid. "What is this?" Hal asked incredulously.

Mab told him, "Flip the switch on the top." Hal reached up and did as she directed. A simple light illuminated the horror inside the tank. The Mariner, bound in chains and stripped of all flesh was encased within. Hal was furious, "The terms of our agreement were that you would present him to me alive!"

Mab waved a hand, "Oh, he is indeed alive, Mr. Sorenson. He is bound with enchanted chains and submerged in salt water and just enough blood to keep him living. The salt water has burned through his flesh making him more…manageable. We had to cover the tank with a cloth because he kept compelling guards to release him with his eyes." In her weird lightning fast movements, she was before the tank and simply tapped on it with her clawed fingernail. "Wakey, Wakey, sleepyhead," she sang.

The skeleton began to stir and

glowing red orbs began to illuminate the cylinder further. Waves of hatred filled the room. The eyes first focused on his captor and then caught Hal's figure and centered on him. The glow became more intense. Fangs began to gnash and click together.

Hal turned to Mab furious, "You know that we will not be able to use him in this condition. We will have to wait for him to heal first. We are going to have to feed the damn thing!"

Mab returned Hal's smirk from before, "Nevertheless, Mr. Sorenson, you did not specify what manner of containment we were supposed to use. You only stated that he had to be alive. As you can see, he is indeed alive... barely."

She continued, "If you keep your end of our pact, The Mariner is yours....after the battle." Hal cursed and stomped around the room and was about to scream at her when the whole room began to collapse with a boom!

Mab grabbed her head and began to scream. Blood poured out of her nose ears and eyes. She had gotten Tethys' message.

It had only taken a few seconds and it was over. The last rays of sunlight poured down from the roof of the cavern. Mab screamed her orders, "Go! NOW! Everyone! ATTACK! We take the battle to the witch! Bring her staff to ME!!"

The tunnels began to overflow with all kinds of creatures. Goblins, trolls, vampires, boggarts, gremlins and other creatures that have names long forgotten. They poured out of the Sidhe like ants coming out of an anthill and ran for Tethys and her army.

"You want me to come to you Tethys! Well, this bitch bites! I have a few more surprises in store for you! I am going to send you into oblivion where you can visit all your other godly relatives that have been banished. You can have a nice little family reunion!" Mab screamed back and jumped on top of the shoulders of a giant mutant dragon hybrid and charged out of the mound.

31 BLOOD RAINED IN HORROR

Tethys was prepared. She stood a good ways out in front of her troops and waited for Mab's ego to bring the fight to her.

The ground began to vibrate with the pounding of an army's advance. The roar could be heard well before anything was seen. The troops tensed and awaited their chance to fight.

In only moments, the attacks began on the outskirts. Mab was trying to breach their ranks by attacking from the side and rear flanks.

Prepared for this, Tethys' troops did not engage but ran toward the middle of the battlefield drawing the enemy to the center.

Vampires poured in from everywhere. Tethys had learned from the last time she was attacked. Salt had been ground into a fine powder and was rubbed into everyone's skin and fur. The vampires' ability to bite and kill was drastically reduced, but that didn't stop them from using claws and other weapons at their disposal.

The Ware's answered the Vampire's challenge. They fought claw to claw. Jace and Joe were fighting furiously, back to back, creating a ring in what appeared to be a vampire convention.

Joe, a cave bear, was taking on three

and four vampires at a time, his massive body simply overpowering them. Standing on his hind feet he was more than fifteen feet tall, his six inch, razor sharp claws dismembering whole limbs with a massive swipe. Should anything get closer, his teeth and fangs made minced meat of anything else. The vampires simply couldn't bite him because of his salted fur.

Though they held the Vampires off, they wouldn't be able to continue with the masses that were attacking them. The vampires were going to simply wear them down.

Seeing the inevitable outcome, Jace threw back his head and howled. An unearthly battle cry was heard by all spirited beings, not just the wolves. Lucky's Werecats and the Werewolves, normally mortal enemies, answered Jace's call. Vampires weren't the only creatures that reproduced prolifically.

From out of the surrounding trees and fields came the Weres, engaging in a life and death struggle till the bitter end. Those able to hold weapons used them, but for most they fought tooth to tooth. Rolling, slashing, biting and tearing until the adversary was eliminated on both sides.

Lucky's band of big cats consisted of Were leopards, cougars, mountain lions, cheetahs and a whole pride of lions. Smaller felines were reserved for guerilla fighting and bait to draw the enemy into traps for their more robust relatives to deal with. They fought on, moving ever so stealthily to the center of the field.

Trolls were actually a more real threat due to their size and age. These trolls had survived a millennia and their bodies had hardened to stone, moving stone. Thankful there weren't more of them - as they were wreaking havoc with some of the other allies. Only the dragons were having some effect.

The sound of battle was deafening. I moved instinctively, my own bloodlust at its boiling point, my swords slicing without hesitation. I felt Jamie fighting to my right, Aundrea to my left and Jean at my back, yelling with glee. I felt Tethys simply swatting away her own attackers, conserving her strength, waiting for Mab.

A giant troll charged in my direction, larger than those gathered together by Brady during the Hell storm. In comparison, they were only training trolls, mere playthings for practice. These things were bigger, meaner, stronger and focused on killing me.

I felt my heart beat in my head; I spread my feet and waited, swords ready. The ground vibrated with the pounding of his feet. He approached - I didn't even blink. He lunged and swung a blow at my head. I ducked just below the tree trunk that was his arm, feeling the swish of air buffeting my back as it went past.

Standing my ground, I resumed my stance and struck upward into his unguarded ribcage with everything I had. My sword hit and vibrated all the way down my arm. Not releasing my hold, I gathered a second breath and heaved, pushing the metal of my blade deeper. Somehow, I tasted the troll blood oozing down my blade and I knew him….One of the first, one of the oldest of them all.

A strength coming from deep inside me poured into my veins. The troll roared in outrage to the pain that I had inflicted. I felt his surprise and fed on his own strength. I knew where he would strike next. We danced, he and I, for what seemed like an eternity. A graceful, beautiful, bloody ballet. With every blow he dealt, I dodged or deflected, turning, twisting and sliced my responses.

It was as if we were completely alone on this field of death. He knew this was the end and was furious to end his days to an opponent so seemingly puny. Struggling with his wounds, spewing blood, he battled on until he stumbled. An opportunity not wasted, I ran, jumped and kicked with all my might, both feet landing squarely into that massive chest, toppling him to the ground. Continuing the momentum, I drove my two swords deep into his eye sockets to sink into his brains. I twisted my blades and his body jerked once more and was finally still.

His children and comrades felt the sudden loss and faltered in their own battles. The dragons, Sam, Max and several other breeds, pressed the advantage the distraction brought and began to turn the tide.

The ground began to tremble anew. Mab, riding some kind of creature encased in armor, part troll, part goblin, part four-legged animal reptilian in nature, like a Komodo dragon with a harness? Charging forward, bringing another contingent of warriors, I knew, somehow I knew, what they were...the black Uruk-hai, her personal army. Trained and cultivated to strike terror.

I began to receive information in my

head, their strengths and weaknesses. Was it Tethys feeding me the information? I couldn't tell, but it seemed many of us were getting the same intel.

Smaller than the trolls, but not by much, there were more of them and they were fast. The Uruk-hai breathed harshly and deeply, and were enormously strong, tense creatures, top-heavy juggernauts with massive chest, neck, shoulder and jaw development.

Consistently surly, they were in the constant pain of their own creation and their only relief lay in violence. Their gait was like walking uphill on narrow poles; as soon as they were created they were locked into heavy plated armor, so there was a perceived sense of crushing weight and momentum to their stride. They seldom stumbled and simply trampled everything they hadn't already killed.

They charged, a fresh enemy advancing on our army, now near exhaustion. As one, we turned to face our newest attackers, our blood running cold, we braced ourselves.

They were lethal, instinctive fighters, much more dangerous than Orcs. They used their wide bladed swords and spiked shields adeptly, smashing and bashing. Their defenses were power blocks - no finesse, no deflections, just brutal power chops that could bounce an attacking weapon back the way it came.

Troy had picked up every weapon he found and fought with tenacity, but nothing seemed right. Swords, knives, dropped spears, lances; they all seemed to feel limp in his hands. He was caught up in the stampede and knocked to the ground. He rolled just in time to evade a lethal chop to his head.

He now prayed for a weapon, scrambling around on his back trying to get his footing to stand. He grabbed at a pole or tree root that was jabbing him between the shoulder blades and pulled and swung. A hammer - or more appropriately a rock attached to a stick.

Thor's hammer!

He jumped to his feet! Feeling exhilarated, he began to bash and mutilate the black demons that were only seconds before trying to end his days.

Those of us not already dealing with an attacker met them. For just an instant, I thought I recognized Lynne, Hawk's wife, among them. I started to move forward and found that I couldn't, something or someone was holding me back. I began looking around and met Tethys eyes. She simply said, "Hold" in my head. I watched the carnage in horror.

The Uruk-hai didn't even bother to defend themselves; they just relied on their armor and moved straight into the attack. They charged, hammering and chopping. Flipping their swords around to use the back-spike to pinion an enemy, or gut them with the prongs on their shields... I watched...I learned...as did we all.

A swath was cut to the center of the battlefield, a direct line to Tethys. We engaged the horror, we wreaked our own destruction, for we would not let our comrades' deaths go unavenged.

Horrific though they were, we met them with our own brand of terror. They chopped and we sliced, they trampled and we overcame. A new energy surged through us all.

Mab rode her mount straight for Tethys, intending to trample her. The animal was halted in its charge, unable to advance, hitting a barrier that smashed its muzzle. Jean changed quickly to gator form, moving quick as a flash and chomped on what was left of him, churning the newly packed earth, digging its own grave as it died.

Mab was thrown as it tumbled and quickly gathered herself to face Tethys alone. Both women circled each other, drawing on the magic's sympathetic to their cause.

A draining feeling came over everything and everyone in the vicinity. Flying creatures battling in the air began to topple to the ground. Ground troops began to fall to the wayside, unable to raise a hand to defend either side - with the exception of the vampires.

They descended, renewed like a hoard of locusts on spring crops. Blood rained as they fed on everything, bloating themselves like ticks. Everyone, including the Fae, prepared to meet our end.

The wind began to swirl into a tornado. A tornado of water! A waterspout! A sweet, saltwater waterspout! A maniacal little giggling voice was heard in the distance, "For you, dear Mother, recharge yourself! How am I to extract my payment if you kill all my debtors?"

I knew that voice...Calypso! She blew in the waterspout! Saltwater burns vamps! Hell yeah! We might just get out of here alive! That was my last

coherent thought as blackness
overwhelmed me.

32 GODZILLA VS KING KONG

They stood facing one another, blasting each other with pure power.

Sucking lightening from the skies, Tethys pointed her staff and struck at Mab and said, "Let's see how you like getting your ass fried!" Mab pulled a blanket of earth in front of her like a shield that absorbed the energy.

Mab blew poisonous powder gathered from belladonna and other such plants, at Tethys dismay. Mab chuckled, "I knew those pixie gardeners would come in handy one of these days." Tethys shielded herself in a bubble of water pulled from the nearby lake.

Tethys retaliated with fire and Mab simply deflected it back to her with the force of pure magic. Tethys stopped the blaze and defended herself from a rain of boulders the size of tanks, pulled from the surrounding countryside.

Tethys raised a large tree and swatted them away like flies. Tethys mumbled, "Hmm...that felt vaguely familiar."

The land rolled and shook; they appeared and disappeared, trying to catch the other by surprise. In power, they were quite equally matched.

With each strike, they pulled on power from the Earth and all the magic it contained, each strike becoming more powerful than the last. They tried every trick they knew. They battled on blow for blow.

A tremendous invisible bomb went off, the shock waves flattening everything within twenty miles. The girls appeared out of thin air. Both Mab and Tethys were flung to the ground...powerless.

Maddey and Adey appeared, their hair flying all around them. They spoke in those weird voices, "We have cut you both off....We are the Balance...We cannot let you exhaust the magic of this Earth...We cannot take sides...You must fight this battle with your own power...Our purpose is to maintain the balance...We have spoken our Lord's will..."

Tethys, realizing that she had forgotten her own way, nodded to the girls and pulled herself to her feet. Their images began to fade and softly they said, "We love you, MaMere, use your training to prevail. Good luck."

Just as their images flickered away, Mab attacked. She used her knife, silvered and poisoned; she lunged for Tethys' throat.

Tethys reached for her staff to find it missing. Listening to good advice, Tethys used her training and turned her body sideways and used Mab's own momentum to flip her over her shoulder into the air.

Cursing and screaming, Mab used her preternatural speed and landed on her feet. She charged Tethys again and met Tethys' boot with her face. She whirled, flinging green blood and spittle to the ground. She swung, trying to backhand Tethys as she pretended to nurse her jaw - and missed. Mab, enraged, flung dirt in Tethys's face and lunged again, landing a couple of good blows. Tethys whirled back to her, slicing her body with the blades encased in her braids and hit her with an elbow to the solar-plexus. She whirled, slamming her left fist to her throat and a responding right round-house punch that crunched Mab's nose and sent her to the ground with a thump.

Mab tried calling out to her minions, to the vampires and anything to help her gain the advantage. Nothing answered that call. She was going to have to do this on her own.

Tethys stood back and watched Mab scream and rant. "I warned you, bitch, and now I am going to teach you the definition of torture." Tethys stepped three steps back, just a foot beyond the holes in the ground and reached for a small black box at her waist and flipped the little switch.

The charges went off all at once. The iron poles shot into the air, the chains caught on the correct catches and an iron net was sprung from above. Hanging from an abandoned crane, Mab had failed to see the instruments of the trap right in front of her. She was caged.

Mab ran to the nearest pole to grab it and her hand burned instantly. She turned to Tethys, "Iron! You built a damned cage!" Tethys laughed, "Yes, and right under your own nose! I am going to enjoy poking you in just the right ways for a long, long time!" Mab screamed, "You bitch! This iron will eventually rust! You can't hold me here forever!"

Tethys was now really laughing, "Correction! That's witch, not bitch…Swamp Witch to be exact. And this isn't just regular iron; I have treated this metal with a new modern chemical process that prevents rust. Leave it to humans and modern ingenuity. By the way, I have a crew that will come out and retreat it on a regular basis for …. Well, for as long as I wish, for they will be the relatives of all that you and yours have slain here this day! You wanted a new home in the sun, well here you go! Enjoy!"

Mab looked up at the iron netting above and at the bars of her cell and smiled. She fell to her knees and began digging furiously. Tethys let her dig. In only a moment or two with her speed and strength she had dug to the bottom and discovered another iron net. Howling in rage she flung herself from her newly dug pit.

Tethys laughed and laughed as she walked away.

33 A KING RETURNS

The battle continued, though hap-heartedly. The vampires had retreated to lick their wounds, the goblins and other Fae seeing their leader in her prison and unable to render any assistance, simply stood waiting for something to happen.

When Tethys and Mab were stopped from draining the Magic, we all began to rouse and regain our strength. Some picked up arms and began to fight the Uruk-hai that remained. Again, seeing their leader caged, they wandered off to only God knows where.

For the most part, the rest of Mab's army laid down their weapons and surrendered, pleading that they were forced to obey her and begged for mercy.

The wounded were being tended to and considerable casualties were covered and carried away. Lucky lost a few of his smaller cats and more than half of his lions. The wolves recorded much the same damage to their ranks.

Leaders of the different clans and races began to converge together. The battle that raged had been masked from the humans by violent thunderstorms blown in from the gulf, another courtesy of Calypso.

So much death and carnage had only taken a mere couple of hours, but would now be remembered for all time. Agreements were made to meet and discuss the implications of what the imprisonment of Mab created in three days time on the little island in Old Lady Lake.

Troy was a different man with his hammer. Sam and Max had flown off somewhere to have a long talk and Hawk patrolled from above, gathering his family together.

Horns honking and blaring came up the little side road. A veritable convoy of all kinds of vehicles arrived. Cars, trucks, charter buses, motorcycles, you name it, and they arrived with much fanfare and dust.

They came, brightly colored, in all manner of attire, most dressed up like rainbows and armed to the teeth. They came running forward to Bataar.

Everyone was completely bewildered. They almost looked human, but if you looked closely, you saw a pointed ear here and there.

One tall young man, who pushed another very old man in a wheelchair, came to the forefront of the crowd. "We made it! We heard your call! We are ready to fight!"

We all started to step forward to try to sort it out, when Tethys put her hands up and stopped us. "Walk away, everyone just walk away. This is for Bataar to deal with."

Very confused, I looked at Tethys and she just smiled. I watched as the scene unfolded. "The young man with long dark hair began, "We heard your call and came to your aid. Some of us have waited for a very long time for you to call us together."

Bataar, increasingly suspicious, asked, "Who are you and what call are you talking about?" The man, a little hurt that he hadn't been recognized immediately replied, "We are your elves - don't you recognize us!" Bataar slapped his head with his hand, "You have got to be kidding me! You are all supposed to be dead, killed by Mab when I escaped!"

The older man stood, not nearly as decrepit as he first appeared, "My King, many of us were killed, but some escaped her clutches and survived, waiting for your return."

Bataar stammered, "How? What?....WHY are you dressed that way?" The young man squared his shoulders and said, "We were celebrating Gay Pride week and we were in the parade when the call came. We got here as fast as we could."

Bataar still confused, "What's Gay Pride?" The older man chuckled and said, "Let me explain. When we escaped, Mab was successful in cursing most of us for two generations. The curse made our women disgusted with their mates. Those that were not revolted at the thought of breeding came to hate the men because they

were used to try to repopulate.
Thankfully, there were some children
born during that time and were only
mildly affected.

We do still have some pure bloods
among us, so our race was able to
survive. Some of the women still feeling
the pull of their maternal instincts even
bore the brunt of mating with the
opposite sex with an agreement of
surrogate parenting in order to produce
Elven children. It is funny; the humans
thought they were the first to come up
with the idea.

But in the interim, a lot of our men
became extremely lonely, being shunned
by most of our women, and began to
turn to each other for comfort and love.
As a result, over much time, most of our
race sort of evolved and those with
Elven blood... and... we identified with
and integrated rather easily into a
human community that prefers same
sex relationships and most of us, though
not all, are, well... we are Gay, or
Homosexual, whichever term you

prefer."

"YOU ARE WHAT!!!" Bataar yelled. Lucky stepped up and whispered in Bataar's ear, "Hold on now, don't judge a book by its cover. I know this is strange for you as a hardened warrior, but take a minute and give them a good look.

They are fit; most have honed and adored their bodies. They move with inherent agility, look closer and SEE what they have to offer. They are used to fighting for what they believe in; you have an army with a strong conviction looking for its leader. What better way to start? All you have to do is train them."

Bataar watched in the distance as some of them came running forward, loping along in a weird gate, holding their arms high, flopping their hands and twisting all about. "Yeah, sure... training, that'll be easy... The hard part will be... well... Oh hell, I am so screwed!" Bataar walked into the crowd to welcome his new family.

34 A LOVE LOST

Hawk searched and found Jace, Joe and Jada. They were a little worse for wear, but the seemed to be ok. They were all about to take off for home when Hawk told Joe to check in on his mother. Joe stopped in his tracks, "What do you mean check in on her! She was here fighting with us, didn't you see her?"

Hawk's face drained of all color and

he had a bad feeling in the pit of his stomach. "I came straight here from the Himalayas. I told Justin to make sure she stayed at home to watch over the others. Where is Justin?"

Jada answered, "Justin is at MaMere's with the girls. I thought Mom was with them too." Hawk shouted, "Go find your mother, all of you!" They all changed again and took off sniffing and searching everywhere. Hawk leapt to the skies, scanning, circling for her familiar form. She had to be in fox form because he had been in the air all day and hadn't seen a sign of her falcon form.

He prayed. He searched. He worried and prayed some more. Under a bush he saw some familiar little feet sticking out and his heart sank. He dove like a bullet.

It was Lynne, his precious little Lynne. Her midsection had been torn out, nearly cutting her small frame in two. She was still alive, barely. She had lost a lot of blood.

He picked her head up gently and her eyes fluttered open. She looked up at him and tried to speak. Blood bubbled out of her mouth, spilling down her chin.

His eyes filled and he called to Tethys for help. His heart breaking to see the one person on this planet that made him feel loved, made him feel like he had a home and a place to belong.

She tried again to speak and he touched her lips and reached out to her with his mind. "Shhhhh... be still, you are going to be ok, just hang on. Tethys is coming and she will heal you."

Lynne whispered weakly, "I love you... its too late... I... hurt... too bad...waited...for...you...Love you always...will... be...waiting... Her eyes dilated and she was gone.

Hawk felt her slip away, her spirit lifting in the wind. He heard one small whisper as her spirit left this world, "Be strong, I'll always be with you." He gathered her torn body to his chest and cried. For the first time since his parents died when he was a child, he cried.

He loved her more than life and now she was gone. He sat there rocking her for a long time until his children found them. Jada collapsed at seeing her mother dead. Jace comforted his sister and Joe went to his father. The four of them sat for some time mourning their loss.

Finally, Hawk laid her body down and rose to his feet. He began gathering wood and brush. His children followed his lead and they made a pyre for their Mother.

When it came time to light the fire, Hawk bent and found some stones and did it the old way. They had wrapped her body in a piece of canvas that was part of Tethys command tent and laid her on the fire.

Hawk sang out in his native language, a song of mourning in Anasazi. The sound was soulful and sad. Justin howled in his spirit voice, Jada screeched as an owl and Joe roared and called out in his bear. Lynne Bordelon Brown-Wing Eschte was gone.

Tethys, Jamie, Lucky and I approached the group and shared in their mourning. Tethys looked at Jamie and me and said, "There may be a chance for a goodbye, but it won't be easy." I got what she was saying.

We joined hands and opened our minds, searching for a spirit that was known to us. Jamie found her first. She was right there watching over her husband.

Tethys blanked her mind and let Lynne enter. Tethys turned to Hawk and in Lynne's voice she said, "Don't be sad, I am here. I won't leave you. I will wait until we are ready to go together. I cannot speak to you, but you will feel me with you always. Where we will go will be a happy place, I have seen it already. Be strong, our children still need you. You have something here yet to do. Remember, I am here with you."

Tethys blinked and the connection was gone. Hawk hugged Tethys, and then reached out for Jamie and me, "Thank you for that. I needed to know she was with me."

Hawk's family encircled him once again and they hugged each other for comfort. We walked away quietly, giving them the privacy in their grief.

35 THE LONG TRIP HOME

It is not known how or why Hawk and his family had been able to change forms to search for their mother. After her death they were unable to change. In fact everyone was unable to change.

The magic that made it possible was still...stuck? Anyone or thing remained in the form they were in when the magic went down. Not even Tethys could change.

Hawk couldn't fly either. So we rented a van and drove back to Dulac. We got Lucky's boat and rode the rest of the way to Old Lady Lake. Jean had to follow them as a gator again. No one talked very much. We all felt the sorrow of loss.

Jamie hoped that the girls would be there and she could reason with them to return the magic to its original state. When they got there they were surprised to find the place in a shambles again.

A war had been fought here and the girls were nowhere to be found. They found Justin and Scratchy curled up on the little couch in what was left of the front room of the house.

Bookshelves were overturned, the contents broken and strewn all over the room. Gouges on the walls both inside and out showed that the place had been defended from an assault on the house.

Attempts to wake Justin and

Scratchy proved hopeless and Cecile sat amongst it all, muttering to herself. She had obviously fought with something, but she was mostly fine.

Tethys sat in front of Cecile and said softly, "Cecile, what happened here?" Cecile kept right on muttering and mumbling to herself. Tethys leaned in closer to try to make sense of what she was saying over and over.

Jace, with his acute canine hearing, started repeating her mantra; clarifying it so others could hear what she was mumbling. "Tell them the secret is in prayer...tell them to read Isaiah's words, forty, twenty eight...Tell them the secret is in the prayer...tell them to read Isaiah's words, forty, twenty eight..." On and on she went, mumbling the same chant over and over.

Tethys sat back thinking. It's a message; she wants us to read a verse from the Bible. Tethys went to the shelf to grab the big Gutenberg Bible and stopped thinking again. She turned and went into the kitchen and got a smaller Bible off her spice shelf.

She looked up at the questioning glances, "What? You try lugging that big old thing around all the time. I got a newer version that was smaller and easier to read." She opened the book and began thumbing through the pages. "Here it is, Isaiah, chapter forty, verse twenty-eight," and she began to read aloud, "*Have you not known? Have you not heard? The LORD is the everlasting God, the Creator of the ends of the earth. He does not faint or grow weary; his understanding is unsearchable. He gives power to the faint, and to him who has no might He increases strength. Even youths shall faint and be weary, and young men shall fall exhausted; but they who wait for the LORD shall renew their strength;   they shall mount up with wings like eagles; they shall run and not be weary;   they shall walk and not faint.*"

As soon as the words left her mouth, a loud sound like a huge bubble had popped and Cecile began to make sense again and rise to her feet. Justin and Scratchy began to wake up as well.

Tethys found her staff lying beside the chair. She picked it up and tapped it on the floor. She instantly changed into MaMere. "Chere, Ah should'a known de answer was with Him, yeah." She screwed up her brow for a moment and her eyes widened in horror.

"Oh, Lord girls, what have ya done!" Jamie surged forward, "What is it? Is it my girls? Are they ok? I still can't reach them! Tell me what's wrong!"

MaMere went to her chair that had been turned on its side and sat it back upright. She sat down carefully and held onto Jamie's hands. "Dem girls are safe, dey is jest fine. Dey has grown into dere power is all, we always knew dis day would come, honey. Dey are gonna make dey own way in de world from now on. You will still see dem from tahm to tahm, I'm sure. You is still dey Momma. But when dey took de magic away, dey took ALL de magic away, dat's what really worries me."

Jamie still anxious and confused, "What do you mean they took all the magic away?" MaMere shook her head, "Chere der is tings in dis world dat is kept hidden by magic. Der is tings that is locked away by de magic to keep de res o' us safe. De girls took away de magic and dem tings got out." She shook her head again and looked at the floor thinking. "Yep, we gotta lotta work ta do, yeah." Jean came up to MaMere with a blanket wrapped around his waist, "You know something Mon Cherie, I never thought the day I walked back into this house I would find it in this condition." He leaned over and kissed the top of MaMere's head.

MaMere looked up at him and leaned into his hand. Her eyes twinkled and everything was good as new. "Is dat betta, Chere? You know we gonna have ta do something about having a young, handsome man kissin on an old woman lahke dese kids' ole MaMere. Mebbe a little more gray hair, a little bald spot even." Jean reached around and hugged her, "Old woman, you don't scare me anymore. Besides, you can just tell everyone I am your young lover. I am sure that will get tongues wagging and more orders for those love potions of yours!"

Everyone was silent and Scratchy had finally reverted fully to Bernice. Lucky went to her and asked if she was alright. She had been pacing, chewing on her fingers, "Blimey! Yes, I'm fine, but I've done a terrible thing. I used da cup ter save da young man's life." Apparently her Cockney English accent had also returned.

Bernice turned to MaMere and dropped to her knees, "That's not all ov da story, Mum. When 'e came back ter life, I dropped da cup thinkin' da vampire was dead. He wasn't. When I turned me back, 'e took da cup an' got a drop ov da blood what was left in it."

Bernice began to sob and MaMere

stroked her head, "Chere, ya jest calm down now, what's done is done." Bernice raised her head, tears streaming down her face, "I'm so sorry, but I was scared we would lose da boy an' i' wasn't 'is time yet!" She wailed.

Lucky walked over to Bernice, "I'll take care of her, she's one of my cats now." Bernice looked up at him, "Blimey! But yew cain' wan' me, I cain' change, I'm worthless ter ya." Lucky smiled, "Anyone that can fight and kill a master vampire that old is hardly worthless. Besides it looks like you are learning to change just fine. You just need the proper motivations."

Lucky pulled Bernice to her feet and wrapped a blanket around her nudity and quietly walked her to the back of the house to change. Hawk had collected Justin and taken him outside to tell him about his mother.

At the sound of Justin's cries of sorrow, Jean asked MaMere, "Do you want to go out there and comfort them?"

MaMere looked out the window, "No Mon Amour, they only need each other right now."

36 PROLOGUE

I sit here trying to hold on to my sanity. I am teaching Calypso how to read. She is constantly frustrated and throws tantrums with the different ways a word can be spelled the same and have different meanings. She reminds me of George Carlin and his famous rants about the English Language. Oh, and let's not forget that she can speak all languages!

The only thing keeping me from strangling her is her eagerness to learn. I thought about getting her one of those speech recognition programs, but she wants to make sure that what she says is printed correctly. I made the mistake of explaining to her what "taken out of context meant" and doomed myself.

Jamie has been reaching out to the girls with her mind, with no response yet as to where they are or what is going on. The only thing she has been able to pick up is a feeling of warmth and love. She is feeling very lost and alone. I try to help comfort her in any way I can.

Tethys and Jean have started taking little sailing trips in and around the Gulf on his ship, newly christened as *A WITCH'S WELCOME*. It was the final touch on their Wedding Ceremony. Tethys kept it together until she saw the ship and burst into tears. Jean is a very happy man right now. They have been taking off every chance they get. It is their way of finding some "alone time". As a result, I have made arrangements to have all of my belongings packed up and shipped to Jamie's house.

With Mab imprisoned, Bataar has also assumed her role as Ruler of the Fae. After the battle, many of those who had been imprisoned or kept under a rule of tyranny came forward and began asking for his protection. He has appointed leaders of each clan as Barons and only unresolvable issues are brought to him to make a determination. It seems to be an amenable arrangement for everyone. Bataar is a fair man and a wise leader.

The Mariner, (Jamie had hung him with the nickname, Ben. She said it was odd saying "The Mariner" all the time. She said he just looked like a Ben to her, short for benefactor.) Ben had somehow been able to revive himself by draining some of Hal Sorenson's followers and was now strong again. He was also sought out by other Master Vampires who wanted to be able to exist without fear of being exterminated. They had their own Covens and wanted to protect them. It was natural for them to pay fealty to their Creator and seek his guidance and approval, if for nothing else but the fact that with the exception of Sorenson, Ben was the strongest.

There were some tense situations when he and Calypso happened to cross paths. They both still hated each other even though they were both on the same team now, so to speak. So they carefully avoided each other. I asked Calypso once if there was anything she could do to free him from his curse. She simply shrugged and said she wasn't the one who cursed him.

Daily training exercises have been arranged for his Elves and anyone else that wished to train. Many of the Fae have joined as well, along with the Weres and even Sam and Max. They realized that in their Human forms, they were vulnerable and needed to be able to defend themselves in any form.

Bataar was reunited with his Daughter. She had been the young scantily clad woman that was drugged and tortured on a daily basis in Mab's throne room. Her husband, the young man chained to her side was made to watch…everything.

He is working with the Pixies and Fairies to come up with a concoction that will help her be free of her addiction to the strong drugs that Mab kept her doped with. The only thing that seems to be working is a few drops of Dragon's Blood that Sam was only too eager to contribute.

Bataar explained to Sam that he was not her mate, but with his training with other Dragons of different races, he has developed a talent for helping them learn to keep calm and focus in stressful situations. He told her that it was hinted at in many of the writings that he had come across concerning dragons that the Dragons of Atlantis had been the only ones to be able to change to human form and had bred with the Atlanteans.

The entire island of Atlantis had

fallen to a great volcanic disaster that burned the island and all its inhabitants. Seeing for himself the capability of the Wyrms, he suspected that Mab had a large hand in orchestrating that disaster.

Since dragons are amphibious and cannot be burned, he suggested that there may be others like Sam and Max that had simply gone into hibernation. He suggested they keep looking for others of their kind. Until then, he would help her with her dilemma regarding her time of breeding.

Max and Splash have a tenuous love-hate relationship. Max wants to rule and Splash cannot be ruled by anyone or anything. Splash, having made her wish carefully, was still able to retain her position with the Nereids. She continually practiced using her legs to walk on land. They found having a representative able to go about on land to attend council meetings and the like and act as a scout for potential threats was an added bonus.

The only real problem was that she was also occasionally spotted by humans. A new cult was forming for those who had seen and encountered "The Creature from the Black Lagoon"! Tabloid stories were constantly driving Joe crazy, having to make sure no credible evidence was recovered.

Things are a little crazy around here, but that's actually the new norm for everyone. Keeping busy with all the new, or maybe I should say Old races of supernatural beings coming forward to be acknowledged, a Council of sorts was formed for the time being to handle all the new changes and situations that had come up. Delegates were selected to represent each race.

Tethys had determined that because she was a Goddess, albeit one limited in powers, was not a suitable leader, but preferred to act as Advisor. Hawk had grudgingly accepted the role as a temporary leader until such time as an official council could be formed with mutually agreed upon rules of conduct, territory establishment and such.

Hawk had spent a while in mourning, soaring in solitude with the spirit of Lynne, until his children had come to him. Joe told him that they needed him here with them. He wasn't the only one grieving the loss of Lynne. To help him come back to Earth, they suggested that Lynne would want him to help those in need as she had always done. It seemed to be working for the most part.

But Hawk would never be the same. He was very quiet and solemn. His anger could be felt just simmering beneath the surface. His eyes always remained the piercing gaze of a predator stalking his prey. He was looking for Lynne's killers. His normally merciful attitude was gone. He was harsh and ruled with an iron fist. Bataar seemed to be the only one who kept him from killing anyone who happened to cause his anger to stir.

We all kept busy with the new changes, but a general feeling of unease was present everywhere. Waiting for the repercussions of what would come to light as a result of the fall of the Magic. We knew something was coming...we waited... we trained... we prepared for the worst. It was coming...and it was going to be bad...very bad.

Characters – Literary and Historical References

The Mariner – a fictional character created by this author and inspired by the poem written by Samuel Taylor Coleridge, The Rime of the Ancient Mariner.

The Rime of the Ancient Mariner (originally The Rime of the Ancyent Marinere) is the longest major poem by the English poet Samuel Taylor Coleridge, written in 1797–98 and published in 1798 in the first edition of Lyrical Ballads.

Tethys - Daughter of Uranus and Gaia was an archaic Titaness and aquatic sea goddess, invoked in classical Greek poetry but not venerated in cult. Tethys was both sister and wife of Oceanus. She was mother of the chief rivers of the world known to the Greeks, such as the Nile, the Alpheus, the Maeander, and about three thousand daughters called the Oceanids. Considered as an embodiment of the waters of the world she also may be seen as a counterpart of Thalassa, the embodiment of the sea. Tethys meaning "grandmother", and she is often portrayed as being extremely ancient

Jean Lafitte -(ca. 1776 – ca. 1823) was a pirate and privateer in the Gulf of Mexico in the early 19th century.

Lafitte is believed to have been born either in France or the French colony of Saint-Domingue. By 1805, he operated a warehouse in New Orleans to help disperse the goods smuggled by his brother Pierre Lafitte. After the United States government passed the Embargo Act of 1807, the Lafitte's moved their operations to an island in Barataria Bay. By 1810, their new port was very successful; the Lafittes pursued a successful smuggling operation and also started to engage in piracy.

Though Lafitte tried to warn Barataria of a British attack, the American authorities successfully invaded in 1814 and captured most of Lafitte's fleet. In return for a pardon, Lafitte helped General Andrew Jackson defend New Orleans against the British in 1815.

Lafitte continued pirating around Central American ports until he died

trying to capture Spanish vessels in
1823. Speculation around his death and
life continue amongst historians.

Mab - Mythologically, Mab was the
Queen of Connact (Queen of the Fae);
the warrior queen of the Ulster Cycle.
She was the combined mother/warrior
aspect of the Triple Goddess. The Pagan
festival of Mabon was celebrated in her
honor each year at the Autumnal
Equinox. During the festival, those
wishing to be King were not endorsed
unless Mab invited them to drink of her
mead wine. This ensured that the male
king would be well versed in feminism
and women's mysteries.

Nereids – In Greek mythology and, later,
Roman mythology, the Oceanids were
the three thousand daughters of the
Titans Oceanus and Tethys. Some of
them were closely associated with the
Titan gods (such as Calypso, Clymene,
Asia, Electra) or personified abstract
concepts.
    One of these many daughters was
also said to have been the consort of the
god Poseidon typically named as
Amphitrite. More often, however, she is
called a Nereid the males are called

Potomoi and usually reside in fresh or brackish waters.

Oceanus and Tethys also had 3,000 sons, the river-gods Potamoi ("rivers"). Whereas most sources limit the term Oceanids or Oceanides to the daughters, others include both the sons and daughters under this term.
Anasazi – A Navajo or Hopi term meaning Those who are not us. Spirit guides.

Agogwe – is a purported small human-like biped reported from the forests of East Africa. It is 1 to 1.7 m (3.3 to 5.6 ft) tall with long arms and long rust-colored woolly hair and is said to have yellowish-red skin under its coat. It has also been reported as having black or grey hair. Its feet are said to be about 12 cm (5 in) long with opposable toes. Alleged differences between it and known apes include a rounded forehead, small canines and its hair and skin color.

Bergrisar- Mountain giant. Bergsrå (Norse) - Mountain spirit. Bestial beast (Brazilian)

Eserinis- Lake Spirits

Uruk-hai - were a larger and more advanced breed of Orc - is one of a race of mythical human-like creatures, generally described as fierce and combative, with grotesque features and often black, grey or greenish skin – a cross between a Troll and a Goblin.

Wyvern - legendary winged creature with a dragon's head, reptilian body, two legs (sometimes none), and a barbed tail.

Characters in this book are all fictitious. Any similarity to actual persons, places or events is pure coincidence.

GLOSSARY

Ah - I

Bauchan – Baw kan

Beginnins – beginnings

Bein – being

Benoit – Ben wah

Bordelon – Bore da lawn

Chil – pronounced chile meaning child

Chirren – Children

Clowder – a group of cats

Dat – that

Delahousse – De La Hoosee
Dem – Them

Demselves – themselves

Dere - Their
Dey – They
Don' – don't

Drippin – dripping

Dulac – Doo Lack

Eart – Earth

Eschte – Esh tay

Fo - For

Fontenot – Fon ten Oh

Gittin – getting

Gladius – Short sword, much like a machete

Hurtin – hurting

Jes – just

Lahk – Like

Las – last

Lengts – lengths

Molly – a female cat, males are called Toms

NOLA – Abbr. New Orleans, Louisiana

Purty – pretty

Robicheaux – Row bee show

Spear of Kira - The Double-Sword is a powerful weapon created a long time ago in the Silver Realm. It has been designed to combine the scope of a spear and the cutting edge of a sword. With fitted blades on each end this weapon, in the hands of an expert, is most devastating.

Ta – to

Tahm – time

Teet – teeth

Thibodeaux – tib o doh
Tings - Things
Tol – told

Tryin – trying

Manger de la merde et mourir asticots
Jean's colorful cursing concerning worms, defecation. "Eat Shit and Die Maggots!"

Wit – with

Wrym – Weerm – mythical creature resembling giant slug

Ya – You

Ya sef - yourself

Yer – Your

ABOUT THE AUTHOR

This is Sonia Brock's second book of her *Swamp Witch Series*. The first book, *THE INHERITANCE OF A SWAMP WITCH*, introduced this colorful cast of characters.

Sonia grew up in Southern Louisiana with her grandparents and her sister Jamie. The two girls were inseparable most of their lives and shared many adventures with their grandmother.

If you would like to interact with the author on her Facebook page at https://www.facebook.com/SoniaTaylor Brock.

Reviews are crucial to the success of books. Please take a moment and let us know what you thought about A Witch's Welcome either on Amazon.com or GoodReads.com
http://www.amazon.com/Witchs-Welcome-Swamp-Witch-Book-ebook/dp/B00AB06S9G/ref=sr_1_4?ie=UTF8&qid=1437005451&sr=8-4&keywords=A+Witch%27s+Welcome